WARDENCLYFFE

Book 1

Lloyd Hall

BRANFORD, CT

Wardenclyffe Series
PO Box 2176
Branford, CT 06405
www.wardenclyffeseries.com

Cover Design © 2021 **Abigail Spence**
Interior Illustrations © 2021 **Minna Ollikainen**

Wardenclyffe/Lloyd Hall. -- 1st ed.
ISBN 978-1-7373919-0-6

Dedicated to my incredible mother, who sparked my love of storytelling with bedtime stories about penguins.

CONTENTS

CHAPTER ONE

THE FESTIVAL

On the day of the festival, I leave my house at noon with my bag over my shoulder. I follow the path north towards the town. I walk by the cafe first. There are no lights on and no noise comes from inside. It is uncommon to see the cafe unpopulated. I can still hear the chickens from the farm on the other side. I continue walking north. The most probable answer is that everyone from the town has congregated in the festival location.

After ten minutes of walking, I hear people. The town is still a mile away but the sound is reaching me. Logically this would mean the festival is loud. I continue walking. There is a banner hanging above the road from the trees. It reads, ILLUMINATION FESTIVAL.

As I continue along the path, the sound of people gets louder. I see the first crowd ahead of me. They are wearing bright-colored clothing and are gathered in front of a wooden stand. A blue-and-white striped fabric tent sits above it. I walk up to where they are located.

"Step right up!" says the woman behind the wooden stand. She holds a small silver ball in her hand. There are bottles stacked on top of each other on a small pedestal behind her. "Who wants to give it a go?" she asks as she tosses the ball in the air and catches it again.

A man steps up. "I'll take a shot," he says.

She hands him the silver ball. He takes a step back and throws it. It knocks over a number of the bottles and the crowd cheers around him.

"We've got a winner," the woman says. She hands him a small metal coin before walking over and picking up the bottles. She carefully stacks them back up on the pedestal. "Anyone else want to try?" Another person from the crowd steps forward. I continue along the path towards the center of the town. As I walk, I hear more cheers from the crowd behind me. I pass a number of similar stands along the road. Each is surrounded by a small group of people.

I stop at another. Mary is behind the counter distributing large containers to the crowd. I look inside the container and see it filled with hundreds of tiny pieces of white material. I approach Mary.

"Glad you made it down to the festival," she says as she notices me.

"What is the material you are distributing?" I ask her.

Mary laughs. "It's food, Bit!"

ANALYSIS – UNKNOWN

"I am unfamiliar with this food," I tell her.

"Well you're not completely unfamiliar. You know the corn we grow up in the fields behind the cafe?" she asks.

"Yes."

"Well that's what this is!"

DATABASE SEARCH – MATCH IN-COMPATIBLE

"It does not appear to be the same," I say. She laughs again.

"No it is, I promise! We just found a new way to cook it," she explains.

"What method of preparation causes the physical appearance to change?" I ask.

"Well, Bruce found us this old book of recipes. If you take the corn kernels and heat them they do this." She holds up a basket of the food. "People seem to really love it." She scoops a container into the basket and hands it to another person at the booth. The person hands her one of the small metal coins.

DATABASE UPDATED

"I shall remember this new information," I tell her.

"You should check out some of the other booths on the way to town! Lots of fun stuff in all of them," she says.

"I will," I assure her. I continue towards the town and encounter more of the booths. Some appear to be other varieties of food while others seem to be games similar to the first booth. Each one has a crowd around it.

I reach the town square at the center of Valentine. There have been a number of changes made since the previous day. The stands with striped tents sit all around and small square pieces of cloth have been strung onto ropes from one side of the square to the other. Dozens more stands stretch out into the field next to the town. Beyond the field, I can see the woods where we installed the lanterns for the finale later this evening.

I wander through the center of the town, past all the stands and people. I hear a voice call out from behind me.

"Bit!" I turn around. Edna is sitting on a bench waving at me. "Come over here!" I walk over and sit next to her on the bench.

"I have finished repairing your holo-recorder," I tell her. I pull the device out of my bag and hand it to her. She presses the button and an image appears above the device of me and a younger Edna. The recording of me speaks, *"I do not comprehend the purpose of this device."*

"Doesn't matter! Just come here," the recording of Edna says. The two of us in the recording lean together.

Older Edna smiles as she watches the recording. "Oh, Bit, look how young we were." She watches the recording play. "Well, I look younger. You look exactly the same as you do today."

"That is because I do not age," I remind her.

"I know that. It's just strange to me, I guess. I've changed so much." She stops talking and we watch the recording together without speaking. People continue to walk by us. Some stop and stare at the holo-recording before continuing to the other stands. The recording stops.

Edna pulls out a small wooden box from her pocket and opens the lid. The box is filled with several small holo-recorder discs. She pulls one out and holds it up.

"These were my mother's recordings. I've never had the chance to watch them." She opens up the holo-recorder and places the transparent disc inside. The image of a young woman appears above the holo-recorder.

"It's snowing today," the woman on the recording says. *"I saw Olivia. She looked sicker. Her dad is trying to find a way to help her get better."* Edna pauses the recording.

"That's my mother, Ava." She looks at Ava's face closely. Ava appears distressed. "She was in love with this girl, Olivia, when she was that age. She never told me that much about her. God, she looks so young in this recording."

I place my hand on her shoulder. I have seen others do this to comfort people. She presses the button and the recording starts again.

"I'm gonna see her soon, though. As soon as she's feeling better. Her dad gave me her holo-recorder to hang on to. I figured I should keep recording things on it." The recording moves away from her face. It shows a small street lined with houses. *"And at least the snow looks nice."* The image moves down the street. More snow is falling around the recording before it stops at one of the houses. It is a tall wooden house with light pouring out of the windows. The recording enters the house and shows the interior. The walls are paneled with wood and the floor is a dark stone. It differs greatly from the building construction I have encountered here.

"Hey, I'm home!" Two figures appear in the recording, a man and a woman.

"Hey, sweetie," the man says.

Edna speaks over the conversation, "Those must've been my grandparents. I never met them. My mom moved down here before I was born. I don't think I've ever seen my mother when she was this age." The recording stops while Edna is talking. "I guess that's all that was on that one." She turns off the holo-recorder. "Thank you so much for this, Bit. You have no idea what it means to see her face again."

Bruce approaches where we are sitting on the bench. "Hey, Edna, mind if I borrow Bit for a little while?"

"Just so long as she promises to come back and see me before the festival wraps up," Edna says, looking at me.

"I promise I shall return before this evening," I tell her.

"Wonderful," Edna says, "I'll be waiting here for you. This is the perfect place for people-watching anyways." She places the holo-recorder into the wooden box and returns it to her pocket. I stand up from the bench and walk over to Bruce.

"Thanks, Bit, I was hoping to get your help with some last-minute preparations," he says.

"I am available to assist," I tell him.

"Oh, perfect!" He waves to Edna.

"What is it that you require?" I ask.

"You know the lanterns you installed?" He leads me away from the center of the town. "We're having trouble getting the final cable hooked into the power station. Any chance you'd be able to help us out?"

"I will assist you with the cable," I inform him. He places his hand on my shoulder.

"That's absolutely incredible, Bit. Do you have any idea how much that's going to help us? You're always doing so much."

"It is how I am programmed," I tell him. He laughs.

"Well, I told Neil to come up and meet us with that truck of his you repaired," Bruce says.

Neil greets us at the edge of the town. He is sitting in the driver's seat of his truck, waving to me. He opens the door and steps out.

"Afternoon, Bit!" He walks over to me. "So you ready to head up to the power station?"

"I am prepared." I walk around to the other side of the truck and climb inside.

"The people up there can show you the cable we've been having trouble with," Bruce says, "and I've got some more things to take care of down here before we're good to go."

The engine rattles as Neil turns it on. Bruce steps back and Neil presses on the pedal. The truck slowly rolls forward along the dirt road ahead of us. We drive along the path to the power station and arrive after seven minutes and thirty-two seconds. Neil stops the truck.

The large metal structure sits in a clearing in the woods to the east of the town. Metal pipes extend from every side of the building, continuing deep into the woods beyond the edge of the clearing. These are the power conduits that connect to every building in the town. Built into the front of the building is a twelve-foot-tall circular door. It is carved with deep ridges that resemble an electrical circuit board. The door has been rolled aside and a man stands in the entranceway.

"Hey, you two," he says as he waves us over. I exit the truck walk over to him. "My name's Frederick."

"My name is Bit," I say.

"Good to see you, Frederick," Neil says. The two of them appear to already be aquatinted.

"Let me show you what we've been struggling with," Frederick says as we enter the power station together. In the middle of the room stands a large cylindrical structure with cables plugged in to various ports. These cables run from this structure to the walls where they continue out through the power conduits.

"I have never been inside this building," I tell him. We walk towards the structure at the center of the room.

"Not too many have. We don't fully understand how the grid works or where all the power comes from. But we know it comes through here." He stops at the structure and places his hand next to a large empty port. "But we found one open port that we can use for the lanterns. We just haven't been able to secure the main cable inside," he explains.

"Where is the cable located?" I ask.

"It's right over there," he says, pointing to a large cable across the room. "But even with ten of us we haven't been able to lift it and connect it into the port here. It's just too heavy."

Neil leans in to me. "You think you can lift it?" he asks.

I walk over to the cable and pick it up. "Yes, I am capable of lifting it."

"Would you look at that," Frederick says.

"Pretty impressive, isn't it?" Neil whispers to him. I walk the cable to the large structure in the center of the room and place it inside the open port, firmly twisting it clockwise. There is a loud click followed by a humming noise.

"The cables have been attached," I inform them.

"Thanks so much for your help, Bit," Frederick says. Neil and I walk back to his truck and climb inside. Neil pulls to release the brake and the truck begins rolling down the road.

"I can't believe Bruce really put this whole thing together," Neil says as we drive away from the power station.

"Why can you not believe that?" I ask.

"Well, it's just massive! I've never seen an event this big before. We've got carts with food, a bunch of old-fashioned festival games, and a whole load of old decorations. Bruce found a book about this thing they used to have called 'carnivals', so I guess he's based a lot of the festival around that."

SEARCHING DATABASE – CARNI-VALS

SEARCH COMPLETE – NO RESULTS

"What are 'carnivals'?"

Neil pauses. "I guess they're kind of like big events where everyone gets together at the same time."

"I still do not comprehend," I say.

"You know, I guess I don't fully either. All I know is what Bruce told me," Neil says, "and he just has such a way of getting people excited about stuff."

"I will attempt to understand more about these 'carnivals'."

SUBROUTINE STARTED – CARNI-VALS

"You should ask Bruce to borrow his book. I'm sure you'd be able to learn a lot from it," Neil says.

"That is very logical," I tell him.

"High praise coming from you!" He laughs. We arrive back at the town and I exit Neil's truck.

"I'll catch up with you later, ok?" Neil says. "I got someplace to be." He drives off towards the northern area of town where his house is located. I walk back to the center square. More people have gathered since my last visit. I see faces in the crowd that are unfamiliar to me.

ANALYSIS

They must have come from other nearby towns to attend the festival that we are hosting. All wear the same brightly-colored clothing.

I walk through the crowd to the bench where I left Edna. She is sitting in the same location as before. I sit down next to her.

"Welcome back." She grabs my hand. "How'd your project go?"

"The project has been completed," I inform her.

"Bruce tells me the two of you put some big event together for the finale?"

"That is correct," I tell her, and she smiles. "I have been assisting with the preparations for this project for three-and-a-half weeks."

"Well I'm looking forward to it," Edna says. "Bruce never does anything halfway." She laughs.

"The finale will be taking place after the sun has gone down."

"Well, that probably won't be too much longer now. You got any idea where he's set this crazy stunt up?" she asks.

"The finale will be taking place at the edge of the field overlooking the valley," I tell her, gesturing towards the field in front of us.

"We should head out for it in a little bit," she says. Edna and I remain on the bench and watch the people from the town move from stand to stand. When the sun gets lower in the sky Edna speaks up again. "You mind giving me a hand, Bit? We should probably get heading over there."

"I will assist you," I say. I extend my arm and Edna places hers around mine. I stand up from the bench and slowly help her stand up with me. We begin walking towards the edge of the field together. Edna walks slowly. Over the past ten years, her walking speed has decreased by approximately twenty percent. As we walk, I hear Bruce's voice coming through all the old town speakers.

"HELLO TOWNSPEOPLE," Bruce says over the speakers. There is a large amount of static in the voice. "THE FINALE WILL BE STARTING IN TWENTY MINUTES. PLEASE MAKE YOUR WAY TO THE EDGE OF THE FIELD."

"I had no idea those speakers still worked," Edna says.

"I was not aware they were functioning either," I tell her.

"Really? It's rare for you not to know something like that," she says. The crowds from the festival have begun to make their way to the edge of the field alongside us. We reach the last stalls. Edna sits down on one of the benches in front of the wooden fence that surrounds the field.

"So what's the deal with those two?" she asks.

"I do not understand," I tell her. She points behind me. I turn around and see Neil and Erin standing at the fence looking down into the valley. They are holding each other's hands. Neil is wearing different clothing than the previous time I saw him. He has replaced his uniform with a dark outfit more closely fit to him. His hairstyle has also been altered to a shorter length.

"There's something there, right? She won't tell me anything," Edna says.

"To what are you referring?"

"Neil and Erin. The two of them!"

"Neil has altered the appearance of his hair significantly," I observe.

"Ah, never mind. You're no fun to gossip with."

QUERY – GOSSIP

What does she mean by 'gossip'? Perhaps I should go ask Neil and Erin since they were obviously the subjects of her question. Before I am able to go ask them about this 'gossip' I see Bruce stand up in front of the crowd. He is on a large platform that has been built for the festival. The sun has now fully set.

"Hello, everyone," Bruce speaks. The crowd falls silent. "Thank you all so much for coming to the festival today! And thanks so much to everyone who helped pitch in. We wouldn't have been able to pull this together without everyone's help." There is cheering from the crowd. Bruce pauses before continuing, "We're almost at the end of our day, but we've got one more surprise here in store for you! I mean, what would the Illumination Festival be without some lights?" The crowd cheers again.

"Well, we've got something incredible planned," Bruce yells over the roar of the crowd. A person next to the platform hands him a large curved horn. I have seen Bruce use this a couple of times before during town events. He takes a large breath and blows into the horn. The call echoes throughout the valley. Twenty-seven seconds later the entire valley is lit up. All of the lanterns that Neil and I had laid out have been turned on. The light pours out of the forest. With all of the lanterns lit up, they form the shape of a flower. Exactly as Bruce had detailed in his drawing. The crowd gasps and cheers when the lights come on.

Fifteen seconds after, there is an explosion from across the valley. Fire and smoke appear from the opposite hillside and a shockwave blows through the crowd, knocking a number of people to the ground. As the explosion happens, the lights go out. Not just the lights from the valley, but all of the festival lights and those in the town square.

EYESIGHT ADJUSTING

"Is everyone ok?" I hear Bruce yelling over the crowd. Erin rushes over to me and Edna.

"Are you two ok?" she asks.

"What the hell happened?" Neil shouts over the screams of the crowd.

The only light is coming from the massive fire on the opposite side of the valley. There is a large crash behind the crowd. I turn around. There is a twelve-foot-tall circular metal shape that has crashed into the field leaving a crater where it landed.

ANALYSIS STARTED

The unique markings allow me to identify it instantly, despite its charred and warped condition.

ANALYSIS COMPLETE – DOOR

This is the door to the power station.

CHAPTER TWO

AFTERMATH

I run towards the power station. Some of the townspeople have decided to follow me through the valley. They are unable to keep up with me as I run. That is to be understood. My body is more capable of moving at faster speeds than the average human. I run along the same path that I laid the cables on two days before. All of the lanterns are no longer turned on.

I stop to examine one of the lanterns. The cable extending from the bottom of it is charred and black. The electrical circuit inside appears to be completely fried. I run forward to the next lantern and encounter the same condition. Looking along the row of lanterns, it appears that every one of them is in the same state of disrepair. I continue along the path towards the power station.

After two minutes of running, I arrive at the clearing.

ANALYSIS STARTED

ANALYSIS COMPLETE – POWER STATION

There is a large crater in the center of the clearing where the power station used to be. I look around and see twisted metal that has been blown out from the crater. I conclude these must be the remains of the building.

The only light in the area is from the arcs of electricity coming out of the ends of wires and the small fires that have started. In the middle of the crater, I see wires that have been melted together from the heat of the explosion. The trees surrounding the clearing have also caught fire.

"Bit, what happened?" I hear a voice scream from behind me. I turn around and see a bright light moving towards me. I step to the side of the light. As it passes, I am able to see that it is Neil's truck. Bruce and a number of the other villagers are standing in the back of the truck. Its lights illuminate the clearing.

"It would appear that the power station has exploded," I inform them. The group of people quickly jump out of the back of the truck. They unload a series of large red cylinders and run towards the edge of the clearing. The cylinders are older model fire suppression units. They are not typically used since there is a limited supply. The last time I witnessed them being used was forty-seven-years-and-three-months ago.

"Yeah, no shit," Bruce screams. He appears to be aggravated. I have not often seen him in this state. He is typically a very calm leader. "Get those in place," he shouts at the other people in the group.

They rush to arrange the cylinders around the clearing then run back to Neil's truck.

"All of you get back," Bruce screams at the group. We step back from the clearing into the woods. He looks around before walking up to one of the red cylinders and pressing the large button on top. A light activates on the unit and he sprints away from the cylinder.

"I said get back," he shouts as he gets close to us. He begins pushing each of us away. There is a hum and the canisters around the clearing explode in a bright white light.

EYESIGHT ADJUSTING

A cloud of smoke expands from each canister, covering the clearing in a white fog. I have never seen this many canisters used at the same time. Typically only one is used per case of fire. The smoke floats around the trees at the edge of the clearing before freezing in mid-air. It reacts with the air and slowly turns from a gas into a solid. Its appearance becomes like a clear crystal block that now surrounds the power station.

The fires and electricity are completely stopped. I look into the large solid structure and see the remains of the power station and the clearing encased inside.

"It appears that you have stopped the fires," I say to Bruce.

"Not now, Bit," he says. I look at him. He is sitting on the ground, leaning against Neil's truck. No one in the crowd speaks. I can hear the sounds of people in the field across the valley.

"I'm gonna head back to the festival and make sure everyone's ok," Neil says as he climbs into the truck. I climb into the passenger's seat and a number of the people climb into the back of the truck again. Bruce does not climb in. He stands up and walks towards the large structure. The lights from the truck refract around the crystal, making it shine.

"Hey," Neil calls out to Bruce, "I'll check in on everyone, ok? I'll swing back in a bit to pick you up." Bruce does not respond, but nods at Neil. Neil starts up the engine of the truck again and pulls away from the clearing, leaving Bruce with three other people who had come to help.

No one speaks as Neil drives through the woods back towards the festival. We pass more of the lanterns. I look out the window. Each one appears to be in approximately the same condition. There is charring along the bottom where the cables had been attached.

The entire forest has returned to its previous state.

We arrive at the field where the festival had been to find it empty. All of the stands that had contained the festival games are now vacant. The street lights are not lit and there is no light coming from any of the windows of the buildings. There is a faint glow coming from some of the areas of the town. As the truck approaches, we see a small crowd. The light from the truck attracts their attention and Neil slows down as they run towards us.

"What's going on?" he asks them.

A woman in the crowd steps forward. "There are fires all over town," she says. "Everyone's trying to put them out."

"Wait, how'd there get to be fires in the town?" Neil asks.

"It looks like all the electrical stuff set it off," she says.

"Damn it, we have to go," Neil says. She steps away from the truck as he pulls it back into gear. The truck moves forward.

"Will you not be able to use the remaining fire suppression units on these fires?" I ask him.

He sighs before responding. "There aren't any, Bit. We just used the last of them back at the power station," he explains. "Those were the last ones we're ever gonna have." We continue driving towards the town in silence.

When we arrive in the center of the town, there are crowds of people running around. Many of the buildings have large fires burning. Neil stops the truck and steps out. I step out after him and look at the town hall. The structure remains intact, however there is light coming from inside. I run to the entrance and open the front doors.

They break apart as I touch them. The wood is black on the inside. I conclude that the fires must have weakened the structure. I look down the main hallway and see a fire. It is contained to the end of the corridor.

Neil enters the building behind me. "How're we going to put this out?" he screams.

SEARCHING DATABASE – RESULT FOUND

"The fire will cease when it has depleted its source of fuel," I inform him.

"Bit, its source of fuel is the town! We can't just let it burn down!" he screams again. He holds his hands in front of his face.

"In that case, you will require a means of extinguishing the flames," I say. He runs back outside and I follow him. He heads towards the fountain in the center of the square.

"You all grab some buckets and let's start getting water onto some of these flames," he yells at the people in the square. He turns towards me. "And, Bit, I need you back in there to help us. None of us can get anywhere near close enough to those flames."

"I will assist you," I tell him. He nods and turns back to the crowd. I walk back into the building. A minute later, one of the people runs in and hands me a bucket of water. I take the bucket and continue down the hallway towards the flames.

ANALYZING DAMAGE

I examine the flames and determine the optimal location to begin extinguishing. I throw the water onto the fire, then walk back to the end of the hallway and hand the townsperson the empty bucket. There is a line of other townspeople waiting at the entrance to the building. I take the next two buckets and continue back to the flames.

I repeat this process a total of thirty-six times before the flames in the hallway have been subdued. Altogether this process totaled three hours and twenty-seven minutes. There are still roughly seventeen small patches of embers, however the crowd now enters the building themselves. My lack of aversion to the heat is a primary difference between myself and the rest of the humans. I walk back outside and see approximately seventy people running between the town's fountain and various buildings with buckets of water. I see Neil standing in the center of the fountain.

"You get those over to the Henderson's place," he yells at one group with buckets of water.

"And you,"—he points at a smaller group—"get over to the south side of town... Make sure none of those buildings are compromised." When he notices me coming out of the building, he steps out of the fountain and runs over. He is wearing all of his typical footwear. This differs from the behavior I typically see from people when enjoying aquatic activities. Often they will remove any footwear before stepping into a body of water.

DATABASE UPDATED – RECREATION ACTIVITIES

I log this information away to ask Neil about at a later time.

"Bit, how's it looking in there?"

"The fire has been extinguished completely. There is significant structural damage," I explain.

"But the fire's out?" He is speaking quickly, which leads me to assume that he is nervous.

"That is correct," I assure him.

"Ok, let's go." He walks towards his truck.

"What is your next destination?"

"We have to go check on the clinic. I don't think anyone's been up that way yet," he says. We climb into his truck again and drive away from the center of the town. We continue east up the hill to where the clinic is located. We arrive to find the building completely unchanged.

"Oh, that's a relief," Neil says. We get out of the truck and Erin runs out to greet us.

"I'm so glad you guys are here," she says.

"How'd this place survive?" Neil asks.

"This structure is no longer connected to the power grid," I inform him.

"How's the solar unit then?" Neil asks.

"It seems to still be working," Erin says, "but it's been having a couple of issues of its own."

"After I have assessed the current damage to the town I will return to assess the repairs required for the solar unit," I tell her.

"Thank god for you, Bit. I really don't know what we'd do without you," Erin says.

I leave the clinic and walk back into the town. The fires have all been put out. I walk past a number of the townspeople who have fallen asleep along the side of the road. I am unsure as to their behavior. The most logical explanation is that they have exhausted their energy reserves by staying awake for a longer duration than usual. I walk past them as quietly as I am able. After years of observation, I have often discovered that waking a sleeping human will result in extreme irritation and oftentimes cases of mild aggression.

I reach the center of the town. The panic from the previous night has subsided. The town is quieter than I have heard before. I look at the town hall. The front door is no longer there. I can see the burned hallway inside. I walk over to the structure and enter, walking down the hallway again. I reach the end that had been on fire only a few hours before. It is now fully extinguished, however much of the structure has been damaged. I walk into the large office at the end of the building. The doors that once separated it are also now gone.

"Hey, Bit," a voice from behind me says. I turn around to see Bruce.

"Hello, Bruce."

He walks into the room. "Guess I'll have to find a new office, huh?" He appears sad.

"That would be a logical choice," I tell him. I have often seen humans use humor to alleviate a sad mood. "I do not believe this building will be an optimal work environment." He smiles but he does not laugh. Perhaps I do not have the grasp of humor that I had thought yet. I will have to do more research.

"I think there are bigger issues we're gonna have to deal with."

"To what are you referring?" I ask him.

He points across the room at the communicator that had been built into the wall. "Do you know what that was, Bit?"

"That is the link to the communicator array," I respond.

"Well, it was. But you see how it's melted?" he says. I examine the melted metal piece. The wires from the bottom are burned.

SCANNING – MATCH FOUND

"The lanterns from the festival are in the same condition," I tell him.

"Not just them, it's everything in the town that was using power."

"I do not understand."

"When the power station blew, everything that was connected to it got completely overloaded. That's what started all of the fires." He walks over to his desk and looks over the charred remains.

"Is there anything that was not affected?" I ask him.

"Nope, if it was electrical it's gone now," he says. "I've been walking around town the whole morning and everything's out of commission." He walks out of the office and I follow.

"Is there anything you require assistance with?" I ask. He shakes his head.

"No, I think I just need to get some rest," he says, walking away.

I proceed out of the town in the opposite direction, following the pathway south toward my house. The path seems quieter than it typically does at this time of day. I am accustomed to hearing people in this part of the town, but no one is outside or awake.

As I walk, I begin to hear people in the distance. I approach Mary's cafe and see a number of people gathered on the lawn. Even more people are inside the structure. I walk up the ramp and enter the building. The tables have all been pushed aside, but there does not appear to be any damage. I look to the kitchen and notice all of the appliances are no longer there.

The room has a series of beds laid out in the middle of the floor where the tables had previously been. I see Mary nearby and walk over to greet her.

"You have rearranged," I tell her. She turns to me.

"Oh, yeah. The cafe wasn't hit as bad as the other places so we're letting some people crash here for now," she says. She unrolls a fabric mat onto the floor and waves at a woman to come over.

"Here, you're gonna take this spot for now," she says to the woman.

"Thanks, Mary, you're a real lifesaver," the woman responds.

"Oh and, Bit?" Mary says.

"Do you require assistance?" I ask.

"No, not me. Edna is out back, would you mind checking on her?"

"I will determine whether she requires assistance," I tell her. I walk over to the back door of the cafe and open it onto the patio. I see Edna sitting on the bench looking out over the fields. The chickens make a lot of noise from their coop below us.

"Come sit with me, Bit." She turns towards me. I sit down on the bench next to her. She is still dressed in her clothing from the previous day. She pulls the wooden holo-recorder box out of her pocket. "It's complete luck that I had this on me. I'm not sure what I would've done if it had gotten lost," she says.

"The data would have been lost," I inform her.

"Not just the data. It's the memories." She pauses before continuing, "I really do hope you see that some day." She opens the box and removes the holo-recorder. She takes out a new disc and places it into the holo-recorder. The disc begins to play and the image appears in the air in front of us.

The image that appears above the holo-recorder is that of Edna's mother, Ava. I recall my memories of her from when I first arrived in the town. I had been shipped to her, however she did not talk to me often while she was alive. She is younger in the recording than I have ever seen her. In my memory files, she was approximately ten years older than she appears in this image. The image of Ava begins to speak, starting in the middle of a sentence,

"... *moved into my new place. Been here a couple of weeks now and I'm finally start-ing to get used to this warmer weather.*" She spins the recording around and it shows the center of Valentine. It looks much newer in the recording. Many of the buildings have not yet begun to collapse.

"*I also met the most amazing guy who helped me move all of my stuff into my new place. He's kinda cute too.*" She smiles as the recording stops. I look at the holo-recorder. The disc has reached the end. Edna opens the device and removes the disc.

"Looks like that was a short one." She places it back into the case with the others. She removes the next disc from the case and places it into the holo-recorder. "Maybe this one will be a little longer," she says as it be-gins to play.

This time someone else is holding the device. Ava stands with a man in the center of town. There is a large crowd surrounding them. She wears a long white dress and he wears a black suit. Bruce's father stands be-tween them and speaks.

"Dearly beloved, we are gathered here today to join these two in holy matrimony..." I recognize this as a wedding service. These do not happen often, however my memory files have recordings of a number that happened in a very similar manner to the one in this recording. We continue watching.

"You know, that must've been my mom's wedding to my father. She used to tell me that they met when she first came down here to Valentine," Edna says.

"Where did she originate from?" I ask. This seems to be a common social question. One to which I never knew the proper answer for myself.

"Well, she never really talked much about her life before she moved here. I only know bits and pieces. But I do think she came from far north."

When the wedding disc finishes, Edna and I move on to another. There is a new voice speaking on the recording. The image shows a small room with books stacked along the walls.

"So... my dad just gave me this new holo-recorder. Not really sure what I should record on it... but I guess I'll just record whatever I want to..." The recording cuts to a new scene. There is a plate of food on the table. The new voice speaks again.

"Dinner time! We're having vegetable stir fry... again..." The video cuts again. This time it shows the interior of a workshop.

"Hey, Dad," the voice calls into the room. A man pops up from behind the desk. His face is blocked by large goggles over his eyes.

"Hey, sweetie, what're you doing here?" he asks.

"Just showin' off some stuff for the recorder," the voice responds. The man laughs.

"And you wanted to record me?" he asks. The camera moves in on his face

"Of course! You're the one who got this thing for me after all!" She laughs as he pushes it away. The video cuts again. It now shows a snowy, quiet street and there is a figure walking ahead of the recording. The new voice calls out.

"Ava, wait up." The figure starts running. The recording follows. It catches up and shows Ava's face before it cuts out again. The disc is finished. Edna does not take out another.

"Do you not wish to see more?" I ask her.

"No it's just, she never talked much about her life before she moved here. She didn't keep anything from then. And she was so secretive about it all. It's just strange seeing all these parts of her life from then," Edna explains.

She takes out one more disc and places it into the holo-recorder. The disc starts up and I see Ava's face even younger than the previous recordings. The other voice speaks from off-screen, *"So tell me about yourself, Ava."*

"Who are you again?" Ava says.

"Olivia! I already told you that!" Olivia's voice says.

"Right, what're you doing?"

"I'm recording everything," Olivia says from behind the camera.

"But why?"

"Well, my dad gave this thing to me. And he's busy with work so I thought I'd keep myself entertained."

"What's he do?" Ava asks.

"Oh, it's boring. He works over at Wardenclyffe. Trying to invent some kind of new power system," Olivia says.

QUERY – WARDENCLYFFE

ERROR – FILE NOT FOUND

"That sounds cool," Ava says.

"It's not," Olivia responds. *"Hey, have you ever been skating before?"*

"No, what's that?" Ava asks.

"Oh, we're gonna have a lot of fun," Olivia says. The disc cuts off again. They do not appear to efficiently utilize the storage available on them for recording. Edna places

the holo-recorder back into the box and closes
the cover.

"I think that's probably enough excitement for today," she says.

"Do you require assistance?" I ask.

"No, thank you, Bit. I think I'm just
gonna get some rest." She closes her eyes.
She is quiet for a couple of seconds, then begins to snore loudly. I stand up from the
bench and leave her to her sleep while I go to
check on the rest of the town.

CHAPTER THREE

VALENTINE

I pull the hood off of an old LAPIN car. It is empty so I move onto the next model. I pull the hood off and toss it to the side of the junk pile. The engine is intact. I reach down inside and feel around the back of the engine block. The fuse is not there.

"Hey, Bit! This the one you're lookin' for?" Neil walks around the corner of another junk pile. In his hand is a small fuse. I take the fuse from him and look it over.

ANALYSIS COMPLETE – T-21 LAPIN

"I am afraid not," I inform him. I show him the markings on the fuse. "This is the T-21 model fuse. I require the T-11 model." I hand the fuse back to him.

"Ah, so close! I'll keep looking," he says. He straightens the jacket of his uniform and runs back towards another pile. I continue to search through my pile of cars. Many no longer have their internal parts. Neil is also unable to find one of the correct fuses. We continue to search through the other junk piles.

"So this fuse will be able to help fix the power up at the clinic?" he asks.

"That is correct."

"Ok good. I'm getting worried about them up there. They've been without power for a few hours already." He walks alongside me as we search. We pull the hood off of the final car in the pile.

"Oh look!" He points inside. "That one looks like it's still got all its parts." I put my hand inside and pull out the fuse. I check the part number.

ANALYSIS COMPLETE – T-11 LAPIN

I place the fuse into my bag.

"I have acquired the part I need for the repair," I inform him. "Let us return to the clinic."

"How long do you think it'll take to fix?"

CALCULATING

"The repair will take approximately two hours to complete upon arrival." We exit the junkyard and continue down the path through the woods. After a few minutes of walking, we arrive at the large wooden trolley platform.

"Trolley should be back in a few minutes," Neil says. "It's great you were able to get it up and running again. It's been such a huge help."

"I was able to use the same solar technology as was used to repair your truck," I explain.

"We're lucky you still had some extra parts left over."

"After installing solar units into the trolley I no longer have parts remaining," I say. Neil is quiet. I look down the tracks and see the plants that have grown up through the metal bars. They have been flattened by the bottom of the trolley. The trees surrounding the tracks also have broken branches from where the trolley has hit them.

I hear the bell from the trolley as it approaches. It makes a clattering noise as it comes down the tracks. I watch it snap the low-hanging branches out of the way as it stops next to the platform. Samuel leans out of the trolley door.

"Hey, Neil, what're you up to out here?" He does not acknowledge me. Over recent interactions, I have gathered that he does not like me. I have also recently observed some of the other townspeople do not want to speak to me at all. Neil does not have such a problem.

"Oh, Bit and I were just grabbing some parts to fix the solar array up at the clinic," Neil says. "Mind giving us a ride back towards town? We're in a bit of a hurry."

"Yeah, sure thing," he says. He moves aside as Neil and I step off the platform into the trolley. We each sit down in one of the wicker seats. I hear the material bending and cracking under my weight.

"Don't mind him, Bit," Neil says as the trolley continues down the tracks. It makes a loud rattling noise as it passes over the plants. Occasionally, I hear a snap from a tree branch as the trolley breaks it off.

"To what are you referring?" I ask him.

"Samuel. It's nothing personal. A lot of people just need somewhere to put the blame for what happened. I just don't want you to feel bad about it," he says.

"I do not feel bad," I inform him. "I do not feel anything."

Neil looks away. "Can't even imagine what that's like. To not feel… anything." We continue in silence for another couple of minutes. I hold my bag on my lap tightly. The trolley stops at another wooden platform and Neil and I exit.

"See you later, Neil," Samuel says. "Good luck getting that solar array fixed."

"See ya, Sam," Neil says. The trolley pulls away. We watch as it continues down the track.

Neil and I walk through the woods towards the main road. The pavement is cracked and plants are growing up through them. A number of old, rusted cars line the path and Neil's truck sits where we left it in the middle of the road. Neil opens the door and climbs inside. I climb into the opposite seat.

"Still feels weird to be in here. Like riding an antique," he says as he pulls the ignition lever. I hear the truck shift into another gear and it begins to slowly roll forward.

"That is because, by definition, it is an antique," I correct him.

"Oh yeah, I guess that's true. Well thanks for fixing it up for me. It's already made it so much easier for me to get stuff to people."

"That is my job," I inform him. We drive by a pile of old, rusted cars.

"If only we had more of the solar panels we might be able to get by."

"The solar panels are in limited supply."

"Yeah I know. Someday we'll have to clean up the rest of this mess," Neil says as we pass by more cars.

"I have removed the essential parts from ninety percent of these already," I tell him. He laughs.

"Nah, that's not what I meant. I meant like the actual scrap metal itself. It's just a bunch of junk," he says. We drive by an old android sitting on a bench. He is in the same place he has been for ten years. He is covered in moss and vines with small parts of his metal body shining through. Further down the road, another android sits against a tree. Her face lies pressed up against the bark. All of the other androids have fallen into disrepair.

"Oh, hold up a sec," Neil says, slowing down the truck. Mary is standing next to the road waving her arms above her head. He stops next to her.

"And where are you off to in such a hurry?" Mary asks.

"Sorry, Mar. We can't stop and chat. The clinic just lost power and we're in a bit of a hurry to fix it," Neil says.

"Oh, hey there, Bit!" she says to me.

"Hello, Mary," I say.

"You gotta stop by! It's been a while since I've seen you down my way," she says.

"It has been two weeks, three days, and four hours," I tell her.

"You see? Far too long! Promise once you're all wrapped up at the clinic you'll stop back my way, ok, you two?"

"I will," I say. Neil nods and presses the acceleration on the truck. We continue away from Mary.

The road rises up along a small hill. The clinic is at the top so it sits above the tree line. This allows for optimal power from the solar panel array. We arrive at the entrance.

"We're here!" Neil says as I exit the truck, however he remains inside. "I'll meet you in there, Bit. I gotta grab some mail for them."

The building leans at an eight-degree angle. Ten years ago, the building leaned at a seven-degree angle. Despite this, it has remained structurally sound. There is a loud yell as someone runs out of the building towards me.

"Bit!" screams the voice. Erin runs over from the clinic and wraps her arms around me. She does not seem to see Neil. She wears the same faded green uniform and cap. The cap hits me in the face. She pulls away. "Thank god you're here. Everything's still completely offline!"

"I have acquired the parts needed to fix the panels," I tell her.

She points at the door behind her. "Oh, thank god."

I follow her out the backdoor into the yard. The solar panels are built into the center of the courtyard and sit on a large rotating platform. I climb up the platform and look over the top of the panels. Half of them are cracked and not functioning. The technology to repair the panels does not exist anymore. If one breaks it is permanently out of commission. Erin yells up to me, "How's it look up there?"

"Half are still non-functional," I tell her. "I will attempt to fix the broken fuse now." I sit down and examine the connection between the ground wires and the panels.

ANALYSIS STARTED

The casing along the wires has dried and cracked off leaving the wires exposed. This exposure has caused them to rust and weaken the connection. I turn off the breaker on the solar panel.

"Yes. I will be able to fix it. However the cables will also need to be replaced soon," I tell her.

MAINTENANCE MODE ENGAGED

I remove the T-11 fuse and set of tools from my bag. Erin remains below as I fix the cable. I cut out the old fuse and begin to connect the new one using my plasma welder. I slowly reconnect the fuse back into the array. The door to the courtyard opens and I hear Erin speak.

"Hey, Neil," she says. I look down and see Neil is carrying his mail bag over his shoulder.

"Hey, Erin," he says. There is a long pause before they speak again.

"So—" The two of them try to speak at the same time.

"No, you go first!" he says. The shade of Erin's face changes to a red hue.

"It's good to see you."

Neil smiles when she says this.

"It's good to see you too," he responds. I stop my work on the fuse and watch the two of them interact. I do not understand much about human interaction. I have tried to observe more to better understand and replicate their actions. They continue to talk quietly to each other and I return to work. After a few minutes, I finish connecting the fuse.

MAINTENANCE MODE ENDED

I flip the breaker switch and the panel jolts back to life with a loud buzz. Neil and Erin jump.

"Oh my god, Bit, I totally forgot you were up there," Erin says. Her face is a brighter shade of red. I return my tools to my bag.

Neil pulls out a small bundle of envelopes and hands them to Erin. I climb down from the platform and walk over. "Bit, I've got to go check in on Bruce. You mind if I take off?" Neil asks.

"I do not mind. I will walk home," I inform him. He walks back through the courtyard door.

"See you later," Erin says. She watches him as he leaves. The door closes and she turns back to me. "So how's it looking up there?" she asks. Her face appears off-color.

"I have repaired the broken fuse. The solar panel is providing power again," I tell her. She wraps her arms around me again.

"You're the best," she says. We walk back inside the clinic.

"The cable will need to be replaced," I inform her.

"How long do you think it's got?"

"My estimation is approximately two weeks."

"Well that's not great," she says. I walk towards the door. "Wait, you can't leave yet." She grabs my arm.

"For what reason?" I ask.

"I need you to help make sure all the machines are back up and running in here too." She points towards the room next to us. "Plus you gotta see Edna while you're here. She told me to send you her way next time you came through."

"I will go assess the condition of the machines," I tell Erin.

"And?" she asks. My brain processes this.

"And I will assess the condition of Edna," I say. She laughs and lets go of my arm, pointing to the doorway with the striped curtain hanging in it. The doorway divides the lobby of the clinic and the rooms of the patients. I step through the curtain. Many of the patients lie in beds. Two doctors in green uniforms walk around and check on them. Edna sits in a chair on the other side of the room. Her eyes are closed. I walk towards her.

"Is that you, Bit?" she asks without opening her eyes.

QUERY – UNKNOWN

"How do you know it is me?" I ask her. I am unsure how she can identify me without seeing me.

"No one else walks as heavily as you do." She smiles and slowly opens her eyes.

"That is because my body is constructed from a denser material than humans," I inform her as I sit down in the chair next to her. She looks at me. Her eyes are foggy.

"Oh I know, you've been saying that since we were kids." She pauses and laughs quietly. "Or at least since I was a kid. I'm glad you came today, I was hoping I could ask you for a favor."

"What do you require?"

"Do you remember this, Bit?" She pulls out her holo-recorder.

"Yes. It is your holo-recorder," I tell her. She hands it to me.

"You and I recorded a lot of things on this when we were younger. I want you to have it. It feels right that you should be the one to take it next," she says.

I turn the holo-recorder over in my hand. "For what reason should I have it?"

"Well you're gonna be here for a long time, Bit," she says. "I like to think that at least this way all those memories will stay alive with you."

I place the holo-recorder into my bag. "I will maintain this for you," I tell her.

"You know, I forgot how much you looked like her until I watched these again."

"To whom are you referring?"

"I think it's the eyes." She closes her eyes. She does not appear to have sufficient energy. I leave her side and examine the machines in the room.

ANALYSIS STARTED

The first machine appears to be operating on a lower power mode. The second one I examine is operating similarly. The oxygen machines are functioning regularly.

I walk out of the room and Erin greets me at her desk.

"So how are things?" she asks.

"The oxygen machines are still operational. Their reserve power was sufficient to function during the interruption. The other machines are operating on a lower power mode," I inform her.

"Oh, that's a relief about the oxygen machines. But what's that mean about the others?"

"They will require additional power to operate at their full capacity," I explain.

"But what does that mean for us?"

"Each machine will only support two people. They no longer have the full capacity to support five patients at a time," I say.

"Wow, that really sucks," she says. She is quiet.

"I will return to attempt to fix the cables of the solar unit," I assure her. "I will require another trip for parts."

"Thanks, Bit, you're the best," she says as I leave. I walk along the path towards Mary's cafe. I can hear birds and cicadas in the forest. After an hour and a half of walking, I arrive at the cafe.

The large structure of Mary's cafe casts a shadow over the road ahead of me. The metal is old and rusted. The building is built into an earthmoving machine from before the flooding. From my research, I discovered it had been used to reshape the land by moving large amounts of earth. The structure is now stationary. Hundreds of years have passed since it was active and it remains as nothing more than a metal shell in the shape of the old machinery. Plants have grown around it and large vines now grow up the sides.

I walk up towards the entrance. The wooden ramp warps under my weight. Above the entrance, there is a new wooden sign which reads, CAFE. One of the many new changes since my previous visit. I step inside through the old metal door.

"The tables have moved," I comment. There are dozens of customers at the tables.

"Yeah, the customers move them, Bit. That's what happens," Mary says as she walks over and greets me at the door. "But we can always move them back if you don't like it." She wraps her arms around me. "How're you doing, sweetie?"

"I am functioning," I inform her.

"Functioning? Not gonna get more than that out of you?" she says, smiling.

"I am well," I tell her. She continues to smile at me as she brings me over to a table. I sit down with her.

"So how're things up at the clinic?"

"The solar unit has been temporarily repaired," I inform her.

"Only temporarily?"

"It will require more repairs soon."

"Well that's a shame," she says. "What else have you been up to?"

"I have restored the trolley," I say.

"No way! That's incredible, Bit!"

"It was simply a matter of acquiring the right components," I inform her.

"Yeah, but that means we might be able to reach some of the other towns for supplies again!"

"You're underselling yourself, Bit," another waiter says as she brings over tea for Mary.

"Thanks, Cindy," Mary says. "So, Bit, apart from the work, how've you been?"

"I am well."

"Yeah, I know. That's what you said earlier. But come on, it's been two rough weeks since we lost the grid. I want to know what you've been up to." She drinks her tea.

"Would you like my diagnostic logs since our last interaction?" I ask her. She laughs.

"No, that's fine. I guess I just have a hard time realizing that you don't really see things the same way as us." I hear loud noises coming from outside the cafe. The sound is that of wood being slammed against metal. Mary looks up at me from her tea. "You know I miss you."

"I have grown accustomed to seeing you," I tell her.

"Now, I think that's the sweetest thing you've ever said to me," she says as she finishes her tea.

"I must continue with my work," I tell her.

"What's next for you?"

"I will attempt to fix the remaining cables of the solar unit at the clinic," I start to say.

"Weren't you just working on that?"

"Yes, however it will require further maintenance to be completely functional," I explain.

The door to the cafe slams open and Bruce runs in. "Bit! We need your help back at the clinic!"

"I do not yet have the parts required to fix the cables. I will need to obtain those parts before initiating any repairs," I inform him.

"No! You don't understand. After you left something went wrong. The whole thing's on fire now!" he yells. I get up from the table and follow him outside.

I see smoke above the trees ahead of us and run towards it. Bruce is unable to keep up with my pace, which is understandable. My construction allows me to move at a much greater speed.

I arrive at the clinic and notice the state of it has been altered significantly since my previous visit. The center of the building has collapsed in on itself. The wood is now entirely black. There are small fires around the structure, but the primary fire appears to have subsided. I walk up to the edge of the structure and can feel a low amount of heat coming from it.

Neil drives up and his truck stops abruptly. He jumps out and runs towards me.

"Where's Erin?" he yells. He climbs over the burnt wood. "Erin," he calls out. I step over the pile of wood into what would have been the lobby of the clinic. I hear a noise from underneath the rubble and remove a beam to find Erin underneath. Neil runs over and helps pull her out, removing her from the structure. Her skin and uniform have a number of burn marks over them.

I walk into the courtyard of the clinic and Bruce runs up next to me. He appears to be completely out of breath. The large metal platform which held the solar units is melted together. Broken metal and glass shards lay on the ground around it.

"Oh my god. Is that the solar unit?" he asks.

ANALYSIS COMPLETE – SOLAR UNIT

"You are correct," I say. I examine the unit to determine the probability of fixing it. "I do not believe I will be able to repair this," I inform him.

"Yeah, I could've guessed that, Bit. There's nothing left to repair." He walks out of the courtyard and looks around the rest of the structure. I can see various objects in piles on the ground, however I am unable to identify what they are.

"Bit, I don't know what we're gonna do without this place." He stops speaking. I walk over to Neil and Erin who are laying on the grass nearby.

"I just… can't believe they're gone…" she says. Tears are coming from her eyes. She puts her arms around Neil and does not speak again.

"We're gonna figure this out," he tells her.

Bruce starts moving around the rubble of the clinic and I assist him in lifting the burnt wooden beams, stacking them next to the remains of the structure.

CHAPTER FOUR

EDNA

The sky is clear today. It has been a week since Edna and the others passed away. Much of the town is gathered in the cemetery for Edna's funeral. I am beginning to understand aspects of this tradition. However, many other aspects still remain a mystery to me. I asked numerous people what the purpose of wearing black garments is. No one was able to give me an answer. I suspect that there is no one alive who knows the reason anymore. There is a lot of lost knowledge.

The cemetery is small and sits on the top of one of the hills outside of the town. It has only existed since the flooding. Most of the older cemeteries are underwater now. The small clearing is packed to the edges. The people are standing close to each other as Bruce stands beside a large hole in the ground.

"Thank you all for being here today," he addresses the crowd. "This has not been an easy couple of weeks for any of us. And losing such a strong member of our community does not make it any easier." He pauses for a moment and then continues, "But I think it is important that we try to remain positive in times like this. And rather than mourning Edna's passing, we should take this time to celebrate her life." There is soft clapping among the crowd. "She has been with us for longer than anyone else here." He stops and looks in my direction. "Well, almost everyone." Some people in the crowd laugh.

The sun is directly overhead. There are still no clouds in the sky. Bruce continues to talk about the details of Edna's life for over an hour before reaching the end. "Now we lay Edna to rest." He grabs a shovel from the dirt next to him and begins to fill the hole as the crowd watches. After twenty-three minutes, the ground has been completely filled in. The people disperse back down the hill towards the town. I walk with them. Bruce catches up to me.

"You know, Bit, without her, that makes you the oldest person here."

"Yes, I am aware of this fact," I inform him. I was activated shortly after Edna was born.

Bruce is quiet. We walk in silence for three more minutes until he speaks again. "What's it like?"

INCOMPLETE QUERY – ADDITION-
AL INPUT REQUIRED

"I do not understand the question."

"To see our whole lives? I mean, you never age, right? You see the whole thing from birth to death. I can't even imagine what that must be like."

I try to process this. "I record all of the events that have taken place since my activation. Is there a specific event that you would like to be informed about?" I ask him. I begin to access my logs about the life of Edna in case that is the information he would like to see.

"No, I just… do you feel anything at all, Bit?" he asks.

"I do not. I am not programmed with emotions," I inform him. His face looks sad upon hearing this.

"Not even today? I mean, you knew her what, eighty years? Isn't there any part of you that is sad she's gone?"

"I—"

SYSTEM PROCESSING

I pause as my brain processes my next thought.

"I have grown accustomed to the routines of visiting her. She has become an integral part of my programming," I say, and he smiles. "It will take time to adjust to a new program without her present."

"See, you always say 'I don't have emotions' but there's something there. Not quite sure what, but you've changed, Bit." We exit the clearing of the graveyard into the woods. The path is heavily worn from travel to and from the hills.

"It is not in my programming to change," I inform him.

"Are you sure, though? I've known you my whole life, Bit. You used to be a lot more mechanical."

"I do not understand what you mean." My internal programming has not been updated since my activation. I am still operating on system OSOLIVE2410. There is no external factor that would have caused this to change.

"Just the way you interact with us is much less rigid. You've picked up pleasantries and actually carry out conversations now. You may not see it but we all do."

"I will run a diagnostic to review my program code from the beginning," I inform him. He laughs.

"There's no need for that. It's a good thing, Bit! It's all a good change." We reach the edge of the woods and he stops walking. The people from the funeral continue to walk around us. He sits down on a nearby bench and I sit next to him.

"Edna left this with me a couple months ago," he says. He pulls out a small wooden box and hands it to me. It appears similar to the other box Edna had owned, however the markings are different. I open the box and see another set of holo-recorder discs. "I think it's only right that they should go to you. You were her closest friend."

I take the discs from him and turn them over. "Thank you," I say.

Neil walks up to us at the bench. I have not seen him in twelve days. He was not in attendance at Edna's funeral.

"Hope I'm not interrupting," he says as he sits down beside us. "I thought I might find you here, Bruce."

"Hey, Neil, what's up?" he says as the two of them embrace.

"Just got back from the southern towns. Parker, Congress, Mesa, they're all out of power," Neil says. He looks down before continuing, "Bruce, the grid is gone everywhere. Whatever we did affected the whole thing." There is silence after he says this.

"What about the solar farms?" Bruce asks.

Neil shakes his head. "I'm afraid not. There are some that're still up and runnin', but none of 'em could support an entire town anymore. And ours is completely gone. It looks like the damage is the worst here, but all the towns are feeling it right now. Whatever was powering the grid for the others doesn't seem to be working anymore."

"I don't know what to do about any of this, Neil," Bruce says. He usually has a very calm demeanor, however he seems upset by this. "How can we survive without power?"

"I couldn't tell you. You're welcome to the solar unit in my truck if you want. Don't know how much good it'll be, but it's somethin'," Neil says. "But I just wanted to stop in and let you know what I found. I'm gonna head back into town with some supplies I got from the other towns." He gets up from the bench and Bruce puts his hand on Neil's shoulder.

"Thanks, Neil. I'll be up that way soon," he says. Neil walks away and Bruce turns back to me. "Well that's unfortunate news. We just can't seem to catch a break."

"Will you not be able to function without power?" I ask him. "I have observed the ways people have been adapting to the limited functionality. Would it not be possible to survive in this manner?"

He shakes his head. "It's not so much the lack of power that's the problem. Most everyone adjusted to not having power in their homes pretty fine. It's what he said about the other towns that I'm worried about."

"I do not understand," I tell him.

He sighs. "We used to have contact with the other towns easily, we had the telegraphs and more ways to get around. Which meant that we could send food or supplies as needed. But without any of that, it took Neil almost a week to get to the next nearest town. Do you see what I mean?" he asks. The connections were still missing in my mind.

"I do not," I say. He sighs again.

"Well, up here, we can't grow as much food as we need to feed the town. Mary grows as much as she can, but most of what we eat comes from the other towns. The climate here just isn't suited for growing food." He walks over and sits down at the bench again. I follow and sit next to him. "And it's not just the food. We also used the telegraph system for so much. It was simple, just old electrical signals through the grid, but it helped us stay in touch with everyone. So now we don't even have a way to communicate with the other towns without physically going there. So if a disaster happens or if we need medicine it could take over a week just for us to get a message to them." He puts his hands on his head. "Sure, we're making do right now. But there's gonna come a time where bad things happen and there won't be anything we can do about them."

He stops talking and we sit in silence. After a few minutes, he speaks again, "Sorry to just dump all that on you, Bit. It's just been rough lately and you're the only one I can really vent to."

"It is ok," I tell him. I look at the case of holo-recorder discs that Bruce handed me earlier. "Do you know the contents of these recordings?" I ask him.

He lifts his head up from his hands. "Nope, but if you look some of them are pretty old," he says as he gets up from the bench. "I think I'm gonna head out now, Bit. Thanks for letting me vent a little. Sorry again."

"It is ok," I tell him once more. He wraps his arms around me tightly before leaving. I watch him join the crowd of people walking back towards the town.

I remove the holo-recorder from my bag and place a new disc into it from the box Bruce gave me. I press the large play button and a new image appears over the device. There is an empty room with rows of small tables and chairs. No noise comes from the recording apart from the faint sound of breathing. Logically this must be the person who is creating the recording. The door to the room opens. The girl I recognize as Ava walks in.

"You know, the whole recording thing was cute at first, but now it's getting a little old," Ava says. *"And since when are you on*

time for class?" She sits down in one of the seats next to the person recording.

"You're not gonna say that when we look back at these recordings years from now," I hear Olivia's voice speaking from behind the source of the recording.

"I highly doubt that," Ava says.
"What've you been up to today?"

"Just helping my dad out in the lab."

"Oh yeah? Doing anything fun?"

"Nah just boring stuff. He's still working on that power cell," Olivia says from behind the camera. The camera leans in close to Ava.

"And what would that be? You know, for those of us who might not have been listening the last time you mentioned it?" Ava says.

"It's just some power thing that's supposed to be able to power the entire grid I think."

"Wait what? That sounds super cool!"

"You think?" Olivia asks. *"I always thought it was kind of boring. Plus don't tell him I told you but I think he's completely stuck with it,"* she continues. The recording cuts off in the middle of the conversation. I shake the holo-recorder. Perhaps there is more of this recording left. I play the recording again and it ends in the same location as the previous attempt. I turn off the holo-recorder. My mind processes the information it just received. Perhaps the father of this girl was

able to create this power cell. The town would greatly benefit from being able to restore power.

I walk towards the town. Many of the people from Edna's funeral are still walking alongside me. After twenty-seven minutes, I arrive at the door of the town hall. The door has been replaced since my previous visit. It is made from unpainted wood, not like the previous door. I knock and a voice answers from the other side.

"Come in."

I open the door and step inside. The floor that had been destroyed by the fire has large planks laid over it. I see Bruce in his office ahead of me. His door has not yet been re-placed. I walk over to him.

"Hey, Bit, you need something else?"

"I require information regarding Edna's mother," I tell him.

"Really? What for?" he asks.

I put the holo-recorder on his desk. "I reviewed one of the holo-recorder discs which contained information regarding a new power system."

"Wait, really? What kind of power sys-tem?"

"I am unsure of the exact nature of this power source."

I play the end of the recording, and Olivia's voice fills the room, *"It's just some power thing that's supposed to be able to power the entire grid... "* I stop the recording. Bruce pauses before responding.

"So this girl's father invented some kind of superpower power system for the whole grid?" he asks.

"I believe that is the case. Therefore I wish to travel to his lab in search of details of this power system or information on how to replicate it," I tell him.

"Wait, but how do you even know it's still out there?"

"I do not. However, there is nothing I will be able to accomplish to repair our current power station. This is the most logical course of action," I tell him. "I require information regarding Ava's previous residence. That appears to be where these recordings were made."

"Bit, do you know how insane it is to travel god knows how far for something that may not even exist?" he asks.

"I am partially responsible for the situation," I inform him. "I am responsible for installing the lanterns."

"No, Bit, that's not on you. You installed them because I asked you to," he says as he puts his head in his hands.

"The time will not pass for me. I will not notice the trip as you would," I inform him.

"No, I suppose you're right. Still, it's a lot to ask of you."

"It is not," I tell him.

"Fine, I don't know much about her, though. All I remember is I think she mentioned living up in one of the northern cities," he says. That is the information I require.

"Thank you. I will depart tomorrow," I tell him.

He stands up suddenly. "Wait! So you're just gonna leave tomorrow?"

"That is correct. I will depart tomorrow at eight in the morning."

"That's so soon!"

"Yes. I believe it is best for me to start soon in order to more quickly restore power to Valentine," I say.

"Ok, but swing by here on your way out, ok?"

"I will," I tell him as I leave his office.

I return along the path to my house to pack my bag with the necessary items for the trip. I arrive at the house and walk inside.

EYESIGHT ADJUSTING

The electricity in the house no longer functions, however I am still able to navigate effectively without it. I have fully memorized the layout of the rooms. I step into the study and walk over to my desk. I pick up the books and return them to the shelf with the others. When I return, I can continue cataloging the information contained in them. I open the drawers and pull out a number of the items I will require for my trip. I remove one of the bags from the back of the door and begin packing.

I include my repair kit, in case I am required to make repairs on myself. I also include the holo-recorder from Edna. This will be useful for identifying the locations in the recordings, as well as any possible information regarding the people in the recording. I close the bag and set it on my table.

Once I have gathered the supplies for the trip, I spend the night closing up the house. I ensure that all of the windows have been fastened, to guarantee that no wildlife is able to enter in my absence. I do not have an accurate estimate of how long this trip will take me. A previous time that I left the house unsecured while on a trip it was occupied by a large owl for a number of weeks upon my return.

I finish closing up the house throughout the rest of the night. When I am done, the sun is rising in the sky. I gather the bag of supplies that I had packed the night before and exit the house. I secure the front door and walk down the path. I stand at the side of the dirt road and look towards the town. I promised Bruce I would see him before my departure, so I head towards the center of town.

I hear a noise behind me and turn to see Neil driving his truck. He stops and leans out of the door. "So you're finally off?" he asks.

"I am leaving for the northern cities," I tell him. He laughs.

"Yeah, I know. Bruce told all of us. I'm here to give you a lift." He leans over and opens the opposite door.

"It is unlikely you will be able to give me a lift to the northern cities. Your truck is not built for the terrain I will cross," I tell him.

"Ah no, as much as I would love to take you all the way there, they really need me here," he says as I get inside the truck and close the door behind me.

"Where will you take me?"

"Well, first I'm gonna take you to the town. There's some folks there that wanna see you off," he says. The roof of the truck rattles as it bounces over the uneven road. Perhaps when I return that will be my next repair.

We arrive at the town and I see a number of people gathered by the now-empty fountain. The base of the white statue is fully visible without the water around it. Bruce stands at the front of the crowd and we pull up beside him.

"Hey, Bit, we got you something for your trip," Bruce says as he walks up to the window of the truck. He hands me a small object wrapped in bright cloth and tied with thin twine. I take the object from him.

"Thank you," I say, as I place the object in my bag.

"We're all pulling for you!" He taps the side of the truck and steps back. Neil starts it up again and drives off. The crowd around us waves as we depart. Neil continues driving through the northern part of town and back out into the woods.

"The path up here is a lot less worn," he says. It is factual. There are no destinations in this direction and, as such, it is uncommon for people to venture this way.

"That is because they do not get used as often," I say. He nods in response. "How far will you be able to take me?" I ask him.

"I should be able to take you as far as the northern bridge. Do you think you'll be able to take it on your own from there?"

"Yes, that will be most helpful," I tell him. The road is completely overgrown with grass in this area. The trees are also shorter and further spaced out.

"Hey, Bit?" Neil asks.

"What do you require?"

"I'm sorry Erin didn't come to see you off."

"For what reason are you sorry?"

"I just mean… she took what happened at the clinic pretty hard," he starts to say. "She just needs some time." After another hour, we emerge from the tree-line onto a large field of tall grass. The truck plows through it, flattening the grass beneath us. I can see two large pillars in the distance.

"It is over there." I point out the structure to Neil.

"Ah, good eye." He turns the truck towards them. "So, do you know how you're gonna get up north?"

"I intend to walk west towards the coastline and follow it north," I tell him. "I have an accurate map stored in my memory."

"Wait, how do you have a map?" Neil asks.

"I have recorded the maps from all the books in the town hall. They have provided an estimated path for me to follow to get to my desired destination. I will also rely on my internal compass for guidance," I explain.

"How long's that gonna take you?"

"I do not know," I tell him.

He is quiet. After a couple of minutes, he speaks again. "You know, I sometimes forget you're not human, Bit."

"Why is that?" I ask him.

"You don't seem super robotic. But I forget that even if you're gone ten years it's not gonna mean as much to you," he says. The pillars are slowly getting closer on the horizon.

"That is correct," I assure him.

"Well, no matter how long you're gone I'm gonna miss you," he says. We reach the base of the large pillars. The two metal spires reach high into the sky and sit at the edge of a large ravine. I open the door of the truck and step out onto the grassy ground. Neil exits the truck and we walk towards the pillars. There is a small metal footbridge that stretches far out over the ravine. In the far distance, I can see the other side with matching metal spires. I walk towards the bridge.

"Wait, Bit!" Neil rushes over and wraps his arms around me. "Come back soon, ok?" he says, then he lets go.

"I will return as soon as I have completed my objective," I assure him. There are tears in his eyes. I turn away and step onto the foot-bridge. I take a few steps and turn back. Neil is waving his arms above his head and I wave my arms in a similar manner to him. I then turn back towards the bridge and continue walking. I hear Neil's truck start up and drive away behind me.

As I walk across the bridge, the metal creaks underneath my weight. I am not concerned. This structure has withstood far more than my weight over its history. I look down below me. The ravine is approximately eight-thousand-feet deep.

It takes me an hour to fully cross over the bridge. I reach the other side and step onto the ground. There are a number of small bushes and grass growing throughout the red dirt. The terrain appears to be entirely uniform for miles. I continue walking. The red dirt crushes into powder as I step on it. There is a soft breeze that blows this dust around the open plains. I turn west and begin walking in the direction of the coastline.

After half a day of walking, I see a series of large objects along the horizon. I alter my path twenty degrees and walk in their direction. A large gateway stands in the middle of the dirt path that I had been following. The sign above it has large lettering which reads, THE SHIPYARD. I walk underneath the gateway. On the horizon, there are a series of twelve metal structures that reach up into the sky. Some of them have cracked in half and the pieces lay next to their original structures.

I walk into the expanse of old metal. The landscape primarily consists of dirt and plains grass with large pieces of metal protruding from the ground. The sun catches the metal, causing a shimmering effect across the whole field. After another hour of walking, I reach the first structure.

ANALYSIS COMPLETE

It appears to have a height of roughly two-thousand feet according to my distance processor. The structure appears to be entirely stripped of any usable parts. Through the frame, I can see a series of staircases that wind up through the building. I walk around the base of the structure looking for any signs of technology. From what I can observe, no part of this structure is connected to the grid.

ANALYSIS – UNKNOWN

My brain is attempting to process the purpose of this facility. The scale of the ships built here would have been miles long. I am also having difficulty processing the way in which these ships would have been transported to the sea. This entire structure is located a great distance from any body of water.

SUBROUTINE STARTED – SHIP TRANSPORTATION

I will continue to run this process in the back of my mind. I hear a noise behind me and turn around. There is a figure approximately 400 feet away from me. The figure is covered in a large piece of fabric that hides their body. They have a large stick and what looks like a bag on their back.

I raise my hand and wave at the figure. The figure remains motionless. I hear a second noise and turn around to see another person in the distance opposite me. Three more emerge from behind the metal structures.

"Hello!" I call out to them. They do not respond.

QUERY

These humans do not seem to respond like the typical people I have encountered. I continue walking away from the first structure towards the next one. The building is similarly constructed to the previous one; staircases on the inside and metal panels covering the entirety of it. I move on to the next structure. As I walk, the people follow me, keeping the same distance away. Each structure takes an hour to walk to.

The third structure is broken in the middle. The upper half sits on the ground next to it. I walk around to the area that would have been the topmost part of the structure when it still stood. There is fine sand surrounding it. I look closely at this different sand. It is clear.

ANALYSIS – GLASS

My brain processes the data. Glass, not sand. I look at the structure. The upper area has large sections that once would have contained panes of glass. The glass would have shattered when the structure fell. Years of weathering must have ground the glass into dust. The structure sits on its side. I look up and see a large room stretching out above me.

I continue walking. The people still follow me while keeping a significant distance between us. As I pass the last structure, I discover a large building attached to the base of it. I walk around and find an entrance.

Much like the others, the interior of this building is empty. There is a sign on the ground that appears to have fallen over. It is a large rectangular sign with letters carved into it. The sign reads, EMBARKATION. The room contains a number of other small metallic structures, however their original purpose cannot be determined. On the opposite side of the room are two more people. These people have the fabric removed from over their heads. Their faces have patterns painted onto them. The fabric around them matches the color of the sand and also has similar patterns painted onto it.

"Are you aware of the purpose of these structures?" I ask them. They speak to each other softly.

LANGUAGE UNKOWN

They do not speak to me, however they point towards the opening I had come in through. Logically, I assume they wish me to exit the building.

I do so and continue away from the structures. I come up to another archway that reads the same as the first one many miles back. THE SHIPYARD. I walk through the archway and continue west. When I turn back, the figures are all standing underneath the archway. They do not pass any further than the edge of the shipyard.

◆

After three days, I arrive at the base of the mountain range. The cliff face is steep and I am able to see a line of trees on top of it. It is also broken up by a number of trees growing directly out of the middle. I determine that climbing this would not be the most efficient means of traversing.

ACCESSING COMPASS

I turn north and follow the base of the mountains. I am searching for a location that will be easier to cross where the terrain is less hazardous. If no such place exists, I will follow these mountains as far north as they will take me.

I turn the corner and find something out of the ordinary. The earth has been completely removed from the mountains and there is a long passageway that has been engineered through it. There are sleek walls that stretch up to the top of the mountains and the sky is clearly visible on the other side. The sun is beginning to set, and as I look west through this passageway the last rays align with the walls.

Next to this passageway, I see an old walking excavator. Just the frame remains, with a faint model number still partly visible on the side. The model number is the same as the unit that Mary's cafe is built into. This one has not been altered in the same way. It does not have windows along the back wall. It does not have the stairs up to the main door. It does not have the CAFE sign. Instead, it is rusted and worn away. These units have been outmoded for centuries. Without anyone to properly maintain them, they have fallen into disrepair.

I walk past the excavator.

ANALYSIS – UNSUITABLE MATERIALS

There do not appear to be any sections within it that contain any parts I would be able to utilize. I step into the passageway. There is a large amount of wind traveling through the tunnel from the other side. My weight keeps me from being pushed back, however my progress is slowed as I walk against the wind.

EYESIGHT ADJUSTING

My eyes attempt to focus and re-adjust to the sunlight directly in front of me. It is overloading my optic units. I close my eyes.

I still feel the wind against me, but I continue on with my eyes closed. My steps are heavy on the ground beneath my feet. Then my foot catches something and I stumble forward. I open my eyes again and shield them from the sun with my hand. I look down at what my foot caught and recognize it as a track.

Upon closer inspection, it appears to be the same model of track we used for our trolleys in Valentine. They are incomplete, though. There are stacks of metal beams and tracks next to those that have already been laid. The rest sit up against the wall of the passageway. I step onto the tracks and continue forward as the sun sets.

EYESIGHT ADJUSTING

Without the sun, the temperature begins to drop.

WARNING – LOW TEMPERATURE

My internal thermometer registers the rapid drop in heat.

I stop walking and sit on the ground. The wind is also causing my body to rapidly lose heat. I begin running as many systems as I can at once.

EYESIGHT ADJUSTING

ANALYSIS – EXTREME WEATHER CONDITION

SUBROUTINE ACCESSED – SHIP TRANSPORTATION

SYSTEM OVERCLOCKED

My internal temperature rises. It has returned to a safe operating level. I get back up and continue walking. The pathway is easier to navigate with the sun down.

After a few hours, it rises again and light pours into the passageway from behind me. I feel my temperature rising as the sun warms me and I cease overclocking my system. There is a loud pop inside my left arm and the entire limb falls limp at my side. I reach the end of the passageway and see the ocean in front of me. It stretches out further than my eyes are able to process.

I sit down on a pile of the unused track rails and empty my bag onto the ground in front of me. I grab the holo-recorder and place a new disc into it, then press play and begin repairing myself.

MAINTENANCE MODE STARTED

I grab my left arm and remove it from my shoulder socket with a quick tug as the holo-recording starts. Edna appears as she looked when she was twenty years old.

"Keep the video on me, ok, Bit?" the recording of Edna asks.

"I will attempt to keep the video on you," I hear my voice say through the recording. I place my arm onto my lap. The recording moves as Edna runs around. She runs in front of the fountain in Valentine. I pull out my repair kit from the bag and open up the diagnostic panel on the forearm.

"Use caution," I hear my voice say as Edna climbs the statue in the middle of the fountain.

"Don't be such a worrywart." She continues to climb. Inside my arm, I see where one of the power converters has blown. I re-

move it as the recording cuts off. I place the blown converter inside the bag and grab a spare. The new converter clicks into place.

MAINTENANCE MODE ENDED

I close up the diagnostic panel and return the repair kit to my bag. I place the arm into my shoulder socket and it clicks into place. I feel the electricity running through my arm as it boots up again and the fingers test their mobility. As my arm is booting, I look out over the ocean. There is a breeze coming from the water and the wind pulls into the passageway. Once my arm has booted up, I grab the holo-recorder and the box and place them back into my bag. I also repack the fabric-wrapped object that was presented to me by Bruce. Then I stand up and begin walking through the trees towards the water.

CHAPTER FIVE

PARADISE

I follow the trolley tracks down the mountainside from the passageway. The tracks sit on the forest floor and are overgrown with plants. Unlike the ones in Valentine, these do not appear to receive regular use. After a couple of hours, I reach the edge of the forest and come to a wide beach.

Beyond the sand lies the ocean that I had seen from the passageway. The water is clear and undisturbed. Small waves wash up onto the shore, and beyond are a number of trees that grow up from underneath the water. The trolley tracks continue out into the sand where they split in two directions. One to my left, the other to my right.

ACCESSING COMPASS

To the right is north. I step onto the tracks and begin walking north along them. The tracks sit only a couple of inches above the sand of the beach. They have equal spacing to the ones in Valentine. After a couple of minutes, I hear something behind me. Far in the distance, down the other direction, I see a rectangular orange object. There is a chiming coming from its direction.

EYESIGHT FOCUSING
ANALYSIS COMPLETE

I am able to discern that the object in the distance is an old trolley. It is traveling along the tracks towards me. I step off the tracks and stop walking. A few minutes later, the trolley pulls up beside me. The bell stops ringing and a large set of old wooden doors open at the side of the trolley. A man in a faded orange uniform leans his head out.

"What're you doing out this way?" he asks, looking around me.

"I am walking north," I tell him as I point along the trolley tracks. He tilts his head at this.

"Where're you off to?"

"I am walking to the northern cities."

He laughs and takes a step down towards me. "To the northern cities? They're hundreds of miles away. What's your name anyways?"

"My name is Bit."

He looks north along the tracks. "Bit, huh? Odd name. Well, Bit, I can take you as far as Paradise, but I'm afraid the tracks don't go much further than that," he says as he returns to his seat in the trolley. He waves for me to enter and I step onto the trolley. He closes the old wooden doors behind me.

"I will travel with you to Paradise," I say. I sit down in one of the seats facing the water. The engine boots up as the trolley moves along the tracks. "I was not aware that other trolleys were still in operation. Did the grid failure not affect your systems?" I ask him.

"Most trolleys aren't running anymore," he says. "This is the last one we still have going. I'm Roger by the way." He taps on the wheel of the trolley. "And this is mine."

"How is this unit able to function? Does the grid still have power in this location?" I ask him.

"Nah, nothing quite like that. This thing's got a solar unit installed up on the roof there," he says, pointing up. "They never actually put this model into production but we found this old thing in a scrapyard and it seemed to run fine."

I look around the interior of the trolley. It is decorated with a deep red wood paneling and trimmed with polished brass. It is incredibly well maintained compared to the trolleys in Valentine. The seats are worn but in good overall condition.

"How is this unit still in such a good condition?" I ask him. "I repair many vehicles and have never encountered one in this state of upkeep."

"We just take care of it, I guess. My whole family has, ever since they found it. We clean it and take care of it. Keeps it from falling into disrepair like everything else."

"That is impressive," I say. I turn back to the water. The trolley moves along the sand as the water rises up over the tracks. The trolley splashes the water to the side as it rolls along. I look north and see a light on the horizon in the distance. "What is that on the horizon?"

"How'd you even see that from here?" he asks. "That's miles away."

"I have extremely accurate vision," I tell him. He laughs again.

"Well, that's Paradise. We'll be there in a couple of minutes."

I look at the amount of light coming off the town. "You have power," I say. The trolley begins to slow down. "The grid is still functioning here." Perhaps the residents of Valentine will be able to relocate to this location.

"Not exactly," he says. "I'll let someone better explain it to you. Not exactly my wheelhouse." The trolley comes to a stop at the end of the tracks. The doors open onto a small wooden platform. A woman is standing outside and Roger walks down the steps to wrap his arms around her.

"How was your trip today?" she asks him. He points back into the trolley towards me.

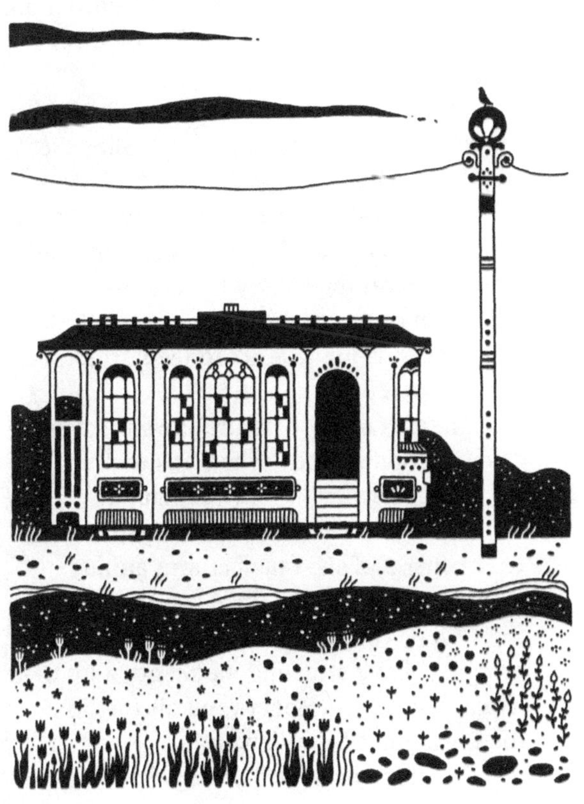

"I picked someone up along the way," he says. She looks at me and steps up into the trolley.

"Hey, I'm Kit." She reaches out a hand. "You come up from Mariposa?" Before I am able to answer her question, Roger speaks again.

"Nah, this is Bit. I picked her up around the tracks near the passageway." She takes a step back when he says this.

"That's the middle of nowhere. What was she doing out there?" she asks Roger. She steps back off the trolley towards him and I join them on the platform.

"She's trying to walk to the northern cities," he replies.

There is a pause before she speaks again. "You're kidding me." She turns to me. "You're really trying to walk that far?"

"Yes," I reply. The two of them look at each other and she puts her arm around Roger's.

"Well, you should come rest at our place tonight. I have a feeling we've got a lot to talk about." She pulls Roger towards the lights of the town and I follow them.

The three of us walk away from the trolley platform down a wide empty street. On either side, I see a series of old streetlights. Unlike the ones back in Valentine, these lights are all still brightly lit. Their light covers the entirety of the street. I walk underneath one and look up at it. I can hear the hum of electricity. There appears to be a significant amount of power running through this entire town.

"What's up?" Kit asks. I look down. The two of them are standing a few feet in front of me. They have stopped walking.

"What is powering this light?" I ask. They look at each other.

"We'll explain in just a bit. It's easier to show you," Kit says. They begin walking again and I follow them. We pass by a number of small buildings, built closer together. Each of them has light pouring out from inside. I think back to Valentine.

SEARCHING DATABASE – NO RESULTS FOUND

Even decades ago we did not have a high enough grid output to power this many buildings. My brain is having trouble processing how this town is able to produce so much power.

We enter the town square. It is similar to Valentine's, but emptier. The town is full of light, however no one is out on the streets. What is the purpose of keeping this much power on when no one is utilizing it? Kit and Roger are walking a couple of feet in front of me. The buildings are all carefully maintained. I can tell they are old, but they still have the appearance of being brand new.

There is a fountain in the center of the town square. It contains a white statue of a figure similar to the construction of the fountain in the center of Valentine. The figure appears to be a different person than ours. The water jets up high into the sky and splashes down around the base. There are a series of lights that illuminate the pillar of water as it sprays up. I follow Kit and Roger as they walk around the fountain, watching the water flow. It is casting refracted light throughout the town square causing small rainbows to appear on many of the buildings.

We exit the square and begin walking down a small hill. There are fewer buildings down this section of the road, however it is still brightly lit by a number of streetlights. The ocean stretches out in front of us. At the end of the pathway there is a small house on the edge of the water.

"That's our place," Kit says as we walk towards the house. Unlike the other buildings, this one does not have light pouring out of it. As we come up to the house I can see more of its details. There is an old wooden porch that rests on top of the sand. The small waves wash up under the wooden boards. There are a number of chairs arranged on the porch facing out towards the water.

"Have a seat, Bit, I'll grab you some water," Roger says. Before I am able to inform him that I do not require water he has entered the house. Kit sits down in one of the large chairs. I follow her lead and sit in the chair next to her. There is a large click and light pours out from inside of the house. I can hear its faint humming over the waves.

"So you want to know where the power comes from, right?" Kit asks as we stare out into the water.

"Yes. I would like to know how the power is still functional here," I tell her. "Do you have an alternate source of power that can be replicated for Valentine?"

"Do you mind if I ask why you're interested?"

"The power source in our town is no longer functional. I am seeking a replacement power source to bring back to our town."

"I see. Do you know what a wind farm is, Bit?" she asks.

SEARCHING DATABASE – NO DATA FOUND

"I do not have any record of a wind farm," I inform her.

"Well, back before the flooding some people tried to use the wind as a power source. They would build these large propellers that would spin with the breeze and generate power," she explains. I have never encountered such a device.

"Where did these devices go?" I ask her. "I have never seen anything comparable to what you describe."

"Most of them got destroyed." She pauses, then points out towards the water. "But there are a couple of them still going." I look out to where she is indicating.

EYESIGHT FOCUSING

I see what she is pointing towards. Underneath the surface of the water, there are small red lights that move in a circular pattern. Occasionally they come up above the surface of the water and I can see that the lights are affixed to the ends of large metal fins.

"That's how we still have power," Kit says.

"I do not understand," I tell her. She laughs.

"Yeah, it's not a common thing for sure. So before the flooding those used to be part of a wind farm. But when the flooding happened they were completely submerged underwater."

"How did they remain functioning?" I ask. She laughs again.

"Well, no one thought they would! Apparently, the people who were living here then were all ready to just give up. But they kept waiting for the power to go out and it never did. Turns out, the water currents and tides kept them spinning. And they've just kept producing power." It takes a second for my mind to process this information. As I am processing, the door opens and Roger comes back onto the porch with a variety of glasses of water.

"Brought you guys some water! Sorry it took a little bit!" he says. He hands each of us one of the glasses. I take mine and hold it. Roger and Kit both drink from theirs.

"Why has this technology not been replicated in other areas?" I ask them.

"Well no one knows how it works," Roger responds.

"Could you not attempt to understand the technology?" I ask.

"We can't just open it up and start messing around with it. We wouldn't want to do anything that might risk us losing it," Kit says.

"Plus we don't really have a way to access them. Most of the turbines are miles under the water," Roger adds.

"We don't do anything that would affect the power systems. We run the exact same number of items every day. No more. No less. That way we don't run the risk of what happened to you," Kit says.

"I am unsure of what you are referring to," I tell her.

"With your power grid. Something happened and all of you lost power because of it," Kit says. "We can't ever let anything like that happen here. If we lost power we'd all die."

"Is there no way to share this power with other areas?" I ask.

"But that could easily overload the system. We can't afford to do anything differently than has always been done here. The power is too important," Roger says.

I process what they have told me. I can see their logic, however it does not align with what I know of the citizens from Valentine. They have a much different philosophy with regards to helping others.

"Why don't we try to get some rest for the night?" Kit says. She and Roger get up from their chairs, and I follow them inside the house. "Here, Bit, you can stay in this room." She opens the door to a room with a small bed in it.

"Thank you," I tell her. She closes the door and I hear her and Roger's footsteps walking away. I place the full glass of water that Roger had given me on the table, then sit down on the bed.

ENTERING SLEEP MODE

◆

SLEEP MODE ENDED

I stand up from the bed and exit the room to find Roger and Kit preparing food.

"Good morning!" Roger says. "You hungry?"

"I do not require food."

"Oh yeah." He laughs. "Well we were just about to head out for the day if you want to come with us."

"Where are you going?" I ask him.

"Roger's going to the trolley," Kit says, "and I'm off to my job at the town hall."

"I will come with you to the town hall," I tell Kit. She is lacing up a pair of boots as Roger cleans the dishes from their meal. Kit stands up and looks at the clock on her wall. She walks over to a large lever next to the door and places her hand on it, then pauses.

"What are you doing?" I ask her. She does not break eye contact with the clock.

"Just waiting," she responds. As one of the hands clicks to the top, the clock lets out a loud chime. At that second, Kit pulls the lever and the power in the house completely shuts off. The hum of electricity goes. "Ok! We should be good to go," she says.

The two of them finish getting ready and we exit the house together. We walk back up the small hill towards the center of town. The streetlights are still lit. We arrive in the town square and Roger and Kit embrace.

"See you tonight," Roger says.

"Not if I see you first," Kit says. They laugh and then part ways. Roger continues along the path towards the trolley platform and Kit walks towards the large building in front of us. The top of the building reads, TOWN HALL. I follow her up the steps and we walk inside together.

The inside of the building is unlike one I have ever seen before. The floors are made from polished marble. There are large lighting fixtures hanging down from the ceiling which brightly illuminate the room. A series of desks line the sides where a number of people sit with papers. Kit walks past all of these desks towards one of the many doors at the back of the room. No one looks up as we enter.

We go through the door and down a flight of stairs into another large room. In the center is a desk with a clock. On the walls, there are a number of levers that match the one I had observed in Kit's house. She sits down at the desk and opens a large book. She flips through a number of the pages until she reaches a blank section, then she looks up at the clock.

"What is the function of your job?" I ask her.

"I'm a power switcher," she says.

SEARCHING DATABASE – NO RE-SULTS

"What is a power switcher?"

"You didn't have power switchers where you came from?" she asks. "No wonder you guys broke your power grid."

"I have never encountered this job before," I tell her. She stands up and walks over to one of the levers on the wall. She places her hand on it and stares at the clock, much like she had done this morning in her house.

"We make sure the power in the town is being used the exact same way each day," she says. The clock chimes and she pulls the lever. She walks back over to the desk and sits down. "That was the power switch for the streetlights. We turn them off at exactly eight AM every morning, and then we turn them back on at exactly six PM every evening." She picks up a pencil and writes in the pages of the large book. "And then I make sure to record every single power switch in this ledger." She spends about a minute writing a new line before putting the pencil down.

"Is it just you doing this?" I ask her. She laughs.

"Oh, no way! It's most of us in this town. This whole building is full of rooms like this. We have a bunch of power switchers like me and then we have all the chimers upstairs."

"What is the purpose of the chimers?" I ask her.

"They're the ones that put out the chimes to all the clocks. Make sure everyone's turning on and off their power at the exact right times. It's a very important job," she says.

I look around the room at all the levers. In total there are thirty.

"How many systems are you in charge of?" I ask her.

"I've got thirty systems that I look after." She gets up and walks around the room, placing her hands on one of the other levers. "This one controls the lights in the library. It gets turned on at exactly nine AM every day and turned off at exactly seven PM every evening." She walks over to another switch. "And this one controls the video screen in the trolley station. On at six-thirty AM, off at nine PM." She continues around the room, placing her hand on each switch, telling me its purpose and times of use.

"That is a number of systems to be in charge of." I look around at all the switches.

"Well, we all work together. Plus we have different shifts so we make sure that the systems are always covered." She sits back down in the chair at the desk, keeping her eyes on the clock.

I remain with her for the duration of the day and observe as she waits for the clock to chime and flips the corresponding switch. She continues this for hours, her mind solely focused on the task at hand. At the end of the day, she walks over to the first switch she had flipped this morning to turn the streetlights off. The clock chimes and she flips the switch back up.

"Well, that's the end of my shift," she says. She quickly logs the switch in the book on her desk and then softly closes it.

DATABASE UPDATED – POWER SWITCHER

We walk up the stairs and back through the main lobby. The desks alongside the room still have people sitting at them, however none of them look up at us as we walk past. We exit out into the town square. The sun has set lower in the sky and the light from the fountain is now the primary source of illumination in the square. We walk over to one of the benches and sit down.

"We can wait for Roger here today," Kit says. "He should be back soon."

◆

The next day I follow Kit to her work again. I watch her run through the same processes as she had the day before. She waits for the clock to chime, flips the switch, then logs it in the book. Her day progresses the same as it had the day before. She flips the last switch and we exit the building. We wait for Roger on the trolley platform today.

The day after that, I accompany Roger on the trolley. He leaves at the same time as the past two days. For his work, he travels down the entire length of the trolley tracks to Mariposa. We wait for about an hour and then begin the journey back along the tracks in the other direction. We pass the area where he picked me up. The entire trip takes the full day and we arrive at the same time as that first day.

I continue this observation of Kit and Roger for a number of days. Alternating between the two of them. I watch them go through the same routine every day. Not faltering from this schedule even by a second. Their lives seem robotic and inflexible.

The end of the day arrives. Kit and I return to the house from the Town Hall. We meet Roger and continue the rest of the walk with him.

"Does anyone ever ride the trolley?" I ask Roger.

He stops walking. "What do you mean?"

"I have never observed anyone riding the trolley in either direction," I tell him. He looks puzzled.

"Well, no one actually rides on the trolley! They've all got to keep to their routines," he says.

"Then what is the purpose of taking the trolley to Mariposa and back every day?"

"That's my routine. It's the same way it's always been done," he says. I cannot understand the logic behind this.

"But the trolley runs on its own independent power unit," I say. Roger starts walking again with Kit.

"Doesn't matter. That's just my assigned routine. Same as my father, the same as my grandmother. Someone's always got to run the trolley." We arrive at their house and sit down on the porch together.

"We all have to keep up the same routines," Kit says. "That's part of what's kept us going all this time."

"Do you not feel stuck?" I ask them.

"Of course not! This is just how we live," Roger says. Kit gets up and walks inside. "The routine is what gives us purpose in our lives. And, most importantly, it keeps us from losing power." I hear a faint chime from inside and within the same second the lights in the house all turn on. Kit comes back onto the porch.

"Do you not feel the need to move forward?" I ask. The humans that I have observed in Valentine are nothing like the people here.

"Not really," Kit says. "I mean, things are running fine. Why mess with that?"

I think about this town. They do not seem to have the desire to help others outside of their own community. I also think about the people in Valentine.

"I think it has come time for me to move on from here," I tell them.

"Wait, why?" Kit says. "Things are perfect here."

"I have made a promise to look for something that would be able to fix my town's power grid," I say.

"But without power they're pretty much doomed already," Roger says.

"I do not believe that they are. And I wish to do all I can to assist them."

Roger and Kit do not speak for a few moments.

"When do you need to leave?" Kit asks.

"I will leave immediately. I wanted to determine if there was any possibility of using the power here to help my town or the people. However, that does not seem like a viable option, so I must move on and look for another solution." I get up from the chair and step off the porch.

"Wait, let us at least walk with you," Kit says. They follow me off the porch and we walk back up the pathway towards the center of town. "So you're gonna keep going up north?" Kit asks.

"That is correct," I tell her.

"We'll go this way," Roger says as he walks down one of the pathways that branch off north from the center of town. Kit and I follow him. This pathway is also lined with a number of streetlights, however it has significantly fewer buildings on it. After a few minutes, we reach a small fence in the middle of the path.

"This is the edge of the town," Kit says. "The path keeps going for a little bit."

I open the fence and step through. Kit closes it behind me.

"Hey, good luck out there. And don't feel like you can't come back and visit," Roger says.

"And don't worry, we'll keep things just the same here for you," Kit says. I turn away from them and walk along the path. I turn to look back and they have begun walking towards the center of town.

CHAPTER SIX

HIGHLAND

I walk along the path away from Paradise. There are numerous streetlights along the side of the road, casting a bright light on it. After eight minutes of walking, the streetlights end, however the path continues and so do I.

EYESIGHT ADJUSTING

The path has a slow upwards incline of roughly three degrees. After an hour of walking, the incline increases to five degrees. The trees surrounding the path have also begun to get shorter the further I get from Paradise.

The terrain is no longer dense soil but now appears to be mostly solid rock. No more trees are surrounding the path. The only vegetation is thick moss growing along the rocks and small bushes that have grown into the rocky terrain. I can see the point ahead of me where the ground appears to start declining. I reach the high point of the land and instead of finding a decline on the opposite side, there is a steep cliff face approximately a mile high. I look over the edge and at the bottom is the ocean with a number of tall buildings rising out of the water. Some of the buildings lean at an angle and appear to have glass along the sides. There are many spots on the buildings that the moonlight is reflecting off of.

I look around to see where the path leads, but there does not seem to be a further continuation anywhere nearby. Beyond the buildings, I can see another cliff face. It appears that the cliffs were carved out around this city intentionally in a circular shape. The shape is too precise to be a natural occurrence.

I begin walking along the edge towards the lower section on the other side. It is approximately ten miles around. This appears to be the optimal route. I take a few steps along the edge until I hear a cracking noise underneath my feet. I look down. The stone appears unmoved so I take another step. The rock cracks away and the entire edge of the cliff begins to slide down into the hole below. I attempt to grab the cliff face, however the rocks slip through my fingers and I fall along with them.

Seconds later, I crash into the water.
SYSTEM COMPROMISED
The force of the fall knocks a piece of my hardware loose, but I cannot accurately determine what. I will run a diagnostic as soon as I am able. My body quickly sinks to the

bottom of the seabed. There are no components inside of me that have any amount of buoyancy to them. The seabed in this location is entirely smooth. I look around.

The surface beneath me is black with white lines patterned along it. Various marine plants grow around me. On the side of the black surface are a variety of buildings unlike any I have seen before. I recognize some as the ones that I had seen the tops of from the cliff. My first instinct is to remove myself from the water before anything affects my systems. I walk towards the closest building, my movement hindered by the weight of the water.

As I walk forward, a large net drops over me and closes in around my body. I attempt to remove myself but the net travels upwards rapidly. After a minute, I am above the surface of the water and being dragged along the side of one of the buildings. I hear voices from above.

As I reach the top of the building, several hands grab onto the net and pull me onto solid ground. The net is quickly removed from around me and I see three people standing above me.

"Who're you?" the tallest one asks.

"My name is Bit," I respond.

"How did you survive that kind of fall?" another asks.

"I am an android," I begin to explain. "My body is constructed to be much more versatile than a human body."

The tallest one nods. "Well that certainly explains why you are so heavy."

"My body is composed of materials—"

He raises his hand. "Yeah we get it," he says. "What should we do with her?" He asks the other two. I look around the top of the building. There are several makeshift structures built into the rooftop. They have been constructed from various scraps of metal welded together.

"Let's get her back over to the prime minister," the third one says.

"Yeah that sounds good." He turns back to me. "Can you walk?"

SYSTEM ANALYSIS – DIAGNOSTIC MODE OFFLINE

STATUS UNKNOWN

"I am unsure," I say.

"Well let's try anyways," he says. The three of them lift me to my feet. My leg appears to be functioning at less than optimal performance.

We walk between the makeshift buildings towards the other side of the roof. I look through the windows as we pass by them. Each building appears to be vacant.

We reach the other side and come to a walkway leading off of the roof and connecting to the rooftop of the adjacent building.

"Be careful crossing. Wouldn't want you falling again," the tallest person says to me. He walks onto the walkway first and I follow closely behind. There is a powerful wind, however my weight keeps me securely on the bridge. The next rooftop has similar makeshift buildings to the previous one.

We continue along five more rooftops, all with the same vacant structures. The last rooftop we come to has a single large domed building in the center. I look at the scraps of metal that make up the building. Many have words printed on them. One scrap reads, STOP. Another reads, ONE WAY.

ANALYSIS – UNKNOWN

"We're here," the tall man says. We step into the building.

The interior is one large room with a variety of seats around the edge. Some appear to be benches, others are wooden chairs, and some seats seem to be the same scraps of metal that the building itself is made from.

A man is standing in the center of the room and others are sitting in the seats in front of him. He stops talking as I am led over. The tall man leans in and whispers something to him.

"Hello, Bit. My name is Rupert. I am the Prime Minister here," he says. He points to the tall man next to him. "And this is my aide, Stewart."

"Hello," I say to them.

"Sorry we haven't been more welcoming. You're finding us on a bit of a weird day," Rupert says.

"For what reason?" I ask.

"We are the last residents of Highland. And today is the day we finally leave this city," Rupert says.

"For what reason are you leaving?" I ask. Rupert looks away from me.

"The city is in ruins, we have no contact with other people, and we can't support ourselves here anymore," Stewart says.

"It is time for us to move on," Rupert says. He turns back towards me. "We must find a new home somewhere out there." Stewart leans in and whispers something in his ear. He nods and turns to the other people in the room. "Friends, the *Elizabeth* is finally ready to set sail." He raises his arms above his head.

The people in the room cheer loudly and walk towards a large door on the opposite side of the room.

"Where are they going?" I ask. Rupert places his hand on my back and leads me towards the door.

"Come see with us," he says. Stewart and the others follow behind us as we exit. Outside there is a ramp leading down to the water below where a large boat is moored.

"Sir, the supplies have finished being loaded," Stewart says as we reach the bottom of the ramp.

"Fine, I'll meet you onboard," Rupert says. Stewart waves and walks onto the large boat. "So, Bit, was it?"

"That is correct."

"Do you want to come with us?"

"For what purpose?"

"Well, you just seem a little lost out here. I can't remember seeing any other androids still up and running in my lifetime." He looks over to the ship. "We're hoping to find a home for us. Who knows, maybe you can find one for yourself too."

"I already have a home," I inform him.

"You do? Then what are you doing all the way out here?"

"I am attempting to locate a new power source for my village," I tell him.

"Seems like a long shot. We haven't had power here in decades. Part of why we're leaving," he says. He turns back to me. "So tell me about your home, Bit."

"My home is a village named Valentine. There are three-hundred-and-forty-seven residents and it is approximately thirty-seven-point-two square miles," I inform him.

"No not that, I mean what's it really like."

PROCESSING – ERROR

"I do not comprehend the question," I tell him.

"Well, did you have friends there?"

"There are a number of residents that I am aquatinted with."

"Oh yeah? Like who?"

"There is Neil the mailman. He often spends time with Erin who runs the clinic. Bruce is the mayor of the town. Mary runs the bakery. And Edna is now deceased," I say.

Rupert smiles. "It sounds like a wonderful group. And I am sorry to hear about your friend Edna."

"For what reason are you sorry?" I ask. Her death was entirely unconnected to Rupert.

"Because losing someone is always sad."

"I do not experience emotions."

"Wow, imagine that."

"I am also unable to imagine," I tell him. He laughs loudly.

"Gee, you sure are an odd duck, aren't you?"

"I am not a duck." He does not seem to be comprehending my function. "I am an android," I say. He laughs louder.

"Well, I'll be sad to not have you along for the trip. Always nice to have some humor on a long voyage. But I do wish you the best on your own journey."

"Thank you."

"But sadly I do have to leave you now. We want to make it out of here by dawn." He puts his arm around me and points towards the cliff on the opposite side of the city. "If you look over that way, there's a large ladder that will get you out of the city. For wherever you may go next."

"I am traveling to the northern cities," I say. He pauses.

"Well, that sure is a far way to go. I think it's too cold there for me personally." He steps forward towards his ship. "Goodbye, Bit. With any luck, we'll meet again someday." He waves an arm above his head. I watch as he walks onto the large ship.

It pulls away from the ramp and I observe as it turns past the other buildings and makes its way out of the cove. The sun has risen higher in the sky. I go back up the ramp to the roof and walk onto the metal platform towards the next building.

I continue to traverse this series of metal platforms and interconnected buildings as I make my way towards the opposite cliff face. Each rooftop has small structures constructed on it similar to the previous ones, however none of these structures appear to have been utilized within recent years.

I reach the final building, which rests next to the cliff face. There is a crude ladder built into the side of the cliff. It appears to be scraps of metal pipes affixed to the stone, leading up to the top of the cliff.

I climb the ladder, mindful to check the strength of each pole as I do so. There is a probability that they were not constructed to support my weight. I can hear some of the pipes making noise. A couple of the thin ones bend as I step on them. The entire climb takes two hours and twenty-seven minutes.

Upon reaching the top of the ladder I move away from the edge of the cliff to avoid repeating the same error from before. I turn away from the cliff and see a large forest stretching out before me.

I walk past the tree-line into the forest. The sun is now high in the sky.

EYESIGHT ADJUSTING

The trees in this forest are significantly taller than the previous trees I have seen. Their trunks are a deep red color and stretch up hundreds of feet above me. The only leaves and branches appear to be much higher up the trees.

There is a path down through the woods with an abundance of plant life growing through it. Within an hour I arrive at a change

in the landscape. The ground dips down in front of me in the shape of a large crater. No trees are growing within this area, however a significant number of flowers are growing within the pit.

I examine some of the plants at the edge. SCANNING MEMORY – UNKNOWN They are species that I am unfamiliar with. I have archived a number of plants from old books in Valentine, however these are not a part of those archives.

I reach out to touch one of the flowers and it begins to glow with a bright blue light. I touch another flower and it does the same. As I walk through the crater of flowers, each one lights up brightly as I touch them. ANALYSIS – BIOLUMINESCENT I am not aware that any species of plant on Earth has these traits. I have only cataloged these traits in various animals and aquatic-based plants. I sit down on a log that has fallen into the crater and pull my left leg up over the other to inspect the joints. DIAGNOSTIC MODE RE-ENGAGED The pressure of the water from before, combined with the continued walking and climbing, seems to have caused strain to this joint. I inspect the knee until I feel something underneath the skin. It appears to be a loose valve within my leg. I open my pack of tools and lay them out on the ground in front of me.

The holo-recorder box is also sitting on the ground next to the fabric-covered parcel from Bruce. I open the box and remove the holo-recorder and a new disc. I place the disc inside and start up the recording. The image of Ava appears again.

"So where are we off to today?" Ava says.

"We're going to explore some caves," I hear Olivia's voice say from offscreen. As the recording begins, I open the panel on my leg just above the knee.

"And why are we doing that?" Ava asks.

"Because it's exciting!" Olivia's voice says. *"Why wouldn't you be excited about that?"*

"Because you're dragging me along on another one of your 'adventures'," Ava says staring directly into the holo-recorder. She also raises her hands and makes a gesture with her fingers as she says the word 'adventures'. It is not a gesture I have observed before and cannot determine its meaning from the given context.

QUERY – ADVENTURES

NO RESULTS

"Oh come on, don't be sour! It's gonna be a lot of fun!" Olivia says. I grab the screwdriver from my tools and start to unscrew the

kneecap covering my joint. The screws each come out and I place them on the ground in front of me. The panel slides off and I examine the joints.

STRUCTURAL DAMAGE

I grab the pliers and start to bend back one of the pistons that is out of alignment.

"Yeah well, that's what you always say," Ava says from the recording. I continue to bend the pistons in my knee back into their proper shape. The realignment must be performed slowly as to not weaken any of the metal.

"And have I ever been wrong?" Olivia says. She is still positioned behind the camera of the holo-recorder so I am unable to see her face.

"No, but this one's so far away. How did you even find it?" Ava says. I finish bending the last piston into place.

"Exploring of course!" Olivia says. She pauses before continuing, *"And I may have found some old notebooks in the lighthouse,"* she says. As I screw the kneecap panel back into place, I hear a noise from within the flowers and lean down to look closer. A small lizard is running around.

"Wait, really? But aren't most of those from before the flooding?" Ava asks. I watch the lizard move through the flowers as I twist the last screw into place and close the panel

on my knee. I stop the holo-recorder, then place all of the items from the ground back into my bag.

I reach my hand down and remain still. After half an hour, the lizard runs close to my hand. It appears to smell me before running off again. I remain still. After another twenty minutes, it returns. This time it crawls onto my hand. I raise it to my face to examine the creature.

SCANNING DATABASE – QUERY IN-COMPLETE

The markings on this creature are completely unfamiliar to me. As I stare at it I notice it has begun to glow with a bright blue light, similar to the flowers around me. I examine the lizard closely. It appears to be vibrating at a rapid pace and emitting a soft humming noise. Its eyes are entirely black and it has not blinked since I picked it up.

I stand up and test my knee with the lizard still in my palm. Suddenly there is a loud crack and the lizard is gone from my hand. I look around to see if I dropped it but it does not appear to be anywhere near me.

STRUCTURAL DAMAGE MINIMAL
SYSTEM INTEGRITY – 97%

Acceptable for now. I will continue to monitor my status. I look around again for the lizard.

RETRIEVING MEMORY – NO DATA FOUND

I do not have any record of the lizard moving. I file the encounter away and continue through the field of flowers.

I reach the other side of the crater and step back into the thick forest. The bioluminescent plants appear to have been limited to the crater. The ones along the wooded path do not share any of the same properties. I stop. There is a large tree on the path in front of me. I look around. To my right, there is a large metal disc embedded in the trunk of the fallen tree.

ANALYSIS

From the look of the tree, it appears to have been cut down centuries ago. New plants have grown up from it. The large metal disc has sharp spikes and appears to be falling apart from rust. I walk around the tree and continue down the path, noticing more and more of the rusted metal discs embedded in trees. Each disc measures approximately 200-feet wide and most appear to be rusted and falling apart.

I hear a noise from above and water begins to fall from the sky.

ANALYSIS – RAIN

The sound of the rain echoes off the metal in the trees around me. I walk underneath the discs and feel the rain stop. I continue along the path and, slowly, the amount of rain increases. The sound of it hitting the metal discs gets louder. I hear a crack from the sky and a bright flash of light appears in the distance.

ANALYSIS – LIGHTNING

The speed of the wind is also increasing drastically. I look around the woods for any kind of shelter from the storm. A lightning strike could cause irreversible damage to my operating system.

I continue along the path, careful to avoid any of the metal discs. The rain soaks me as I walk. Another bright flash of light and a loud crack quickly after. Based on the pause between the flash of light and the noise, I estimate the storm to be roughly 2.7 miles away from my current location and approaching quickly.

I increase my pace. I also look around the woods for anything that can shelter me effectively from the storm. Another flash of light and the crack of thunder follows. 1.3 miles this time. It's almost on top of me.

Another flash of light, within yards this time. The sound happens instantaneously.

EYESIGHT ADJUSTING

I am unable to see. Another crack of thunder from—

SYSTEM OVERLOAD

What is happening? My vision is still not online.

HARDWARE MALFUNCTION – CRIT-
ICAL STATE
My system checks appear—
ENTERING SAFETY MODE – ALL
SYSTEMS SHUT DOWN

CHAPTER SEVEN

ST. HELENS

SYSTEM REBOOTING
—to be functioning normally.
SYSTEMS CHECK
What happened to me?
RUNNING DIAGNOSTIC TEST
There was a battery overload. I am unable
to see.
EYESIGHT RE-ENGAGING
ANALYSIS
I am surrounded by a thick cloth material.
I can feel myself moving up and down steadi-
ly. I attempt to move my limbs but am hin-
dered by the fabric. In addition to the cloth,
there are also a number of large metal pieces
surrounding me. This does not appear to be
the forest that I had been in previously.
HARDWARE REBOOT IN PROGRESS.
My arms successfully reboot, however
my legs still appear to be inoperable.

"Hello?" I say. As soon as I have spoken, I feel myself fall approximately five feet and crash into the ground. There is silence.

"I require assistance," I explain. I hear a noise beyond the cloth. Suddenly it is removed and I see a girl standing above me. She does not say anything.

"My hardware appears to not be responding to my reboot process," I explain.

"What are you?" the girl asks.

"I am an android." I attempt to pull myself upright as we talk. As I do, the girl takes a step back from me.

"But you're just scrap metal." She leans in closer.

"I am constructed from metal. However I do not believe it would be considered scrap," I explain. There is silence after I say this.

"But you were just lying there on the ground."

"My systems were overloaded due to the storm."

"What storm?" she asks. I look around and the ground appears to be completely dry.

ANALYSIS

My systems appear to have been offline for a significant amount of time.

"I've never seen a working android before," she says.

"I have not encountered another working android in forty-five years," I say.

"Wait really?" She looks surprised.

"Yes. My construction was much more advanced than the previous models. The battery units on many had a limited capacity."

"So what, you've just got a better battery than them?"

"That is correct. My battery capacity far exceeds the standard android," I explain. There is silence again between us. "My name is Bit."

"You have a name?" Her expression changes.

"Do you not?" I ask. She smiles slightly.

"No I do, it's Jasmine. Where'd you get a name like Bit anyways?"

"It was the name assigned to me."

"Assigned? What do you mean?"

"When I was created, the name was left inside my memory files." I try to stand up again, however my legs do not respond.

SYSTEM REBOOT ERROR

I look around for my bag and notice it on her shoulder.

"You are carrying my bag."

"What, this? I thought it was just more scrap."

"It contains my repair kit. I will require that to make adequate repairs to my system." I look around us. I am in a different location than I had been previously. "What location is this?"

"How can you not know where you are? These are the Red Woods," she explains.

SEARCHING DATABASE – NO RE-SULTS

"I am unfamiliar with this location."

She sits down in front of me. "What were you even doing out here in the first place?" She crosses her legs and stares at me.

"I am traveling north," I explain.

"Like on an adventure?"

QUERY – ADVENTURE

I have heard this term before, however I do not yet fully understand its meaning.

"Would you please define 'adventure'?" I ask. She looks confused.

"I've never really had to define it before. I guess it's like going out and seeing the world. Seeing new places, you know? Trying to find something new." My brain processes this.

DATABASE UPDATED – ADVEN-TURE

"I am on an adventure," I tell her.

"So then what's your adventure?" she asks.

"I am seeking information about a power system in the northern cities," I tell her.

"Wait, you're going all the way up to northern cities?"

"That is correct."

"But that's so far away! And I've heard it's really cold up there!"

"That is also correct," I tell her.

"Do you even know which one you're going to?"

SCANNING MEMORY – NO RESULTS FOUND

"I do not," I tell her.

"I've heard the biggest city up there is called June. But I've never gone that far from home." She does not speak for another minute after this. We sit in silence as I wait for my legs to reboot.

SYSTEM REBOOT ERROR

"My legs are not functioning. I will need to repair them."

"Well I was going to take you back to my village."

"What is the name of your village?"

"It's called St. Helens."

"Did your village also lose power when the grid was disrupted?"

"Oh no, we've never been connected to the grid." I recall Paradise in my memories. Perhaps this new village also has an independent power source.

"Where does your source of power for the village come from?"

"We don't have power," she says. I attempt to process this.

"You do not use electricity?"

"Nope, we've been off the grid for generations now."

"I have never encountered anyone who does not function with electricity."

"Yeah, people aren't really a fan of any kind of technology there." She pauses. "I'm actually not sure how they're going to react to you being there."

"For what reason?"

"Well, you're technology. We're used to just melting all old tech down," she says.

"For what purpose do you melt technology down?"

"That's just how it is. We melt down scrap metal and use it to make tools and supplies for other towns."

"Are you intending to melt me down?" I ask.

"I mean I was going to, but now I'm not really sure." She stands up and paces around.

"I do not fit your definition of scrap metal," I say. She stops walking.

"I guess you've got a point. Maybe I can convince my dad to help you out." She grabs the fabric from around me and pulls me up onto her back. The other metal in the bag scrapes against me. This time, however, she keeps my head outside the bag so I am able to see the surroundings. Jasmine walks down the path through the woods.

"These trees have grown much higher than the ones south of here," I say.

"Oh yeah, that's why I like to come up this way to collect scrap. The whole forest is just so beautiful."

QUERY – BEAUTIFUL

"What is beautiful?" I ask.

"Oh come on, you must know what beauty is," she says.

"I am aware of the definition of the word. However I do not understand what makes something beautiful," I tell her.

"That's a tough one. It's a little different for everyone." She pauses for a few minutes, continuing to carry me through the woods. Based on the sun, I determine we are still traveling north. "Sometimes it's about memories. Like something is beautiful because it reminds us of a happy memory. Sometimes it's an aesthetic. Lines, shapes, and colors that are pleasing to the eye," she explains.

"I will attempt to create a subroutine for recognizing beauty," I say.

SUBROUTINE CREATED – BEAUTY
SUBROUTINE UPDATED – BEAUTY

"You know, you're probably one of the oddest things I've met," she says. There is a large hill in front of us that she begins to walk up. I am unable to see over the top from the angle I am being held at. As she reaches the crest of the hill, I am able to see.

There is a large lake stretching out for miles in every direction. In the center is an island that seems to be overgrown with a variety of plants and trees that do not match any I have previously seen.

"There it is," Jasmine says. "Welcome to St. Helens."

She continues along the pathway and down the small hill towards the edge of the lake. I attempt to look around and observe the area, but I am hindered by being inside the fabric bag. As we approach the water, I notice a series of small wooden boats.

"There is no sand," I observe. Typically there is sand near any large body of water, but this water is surrounded by grass and other vegetation that appears to continue into the water.

"Yeah, you're not going to find too much sand around here. We're pretty far away from the coastline," Jasmine says. We reach one of the boats and she drops me onto the ground along with the rest of the metal. "I'm just gonna put you down for a second while I get one of these ready," she explains.

I observe as she flips one of the boats upwards and turns a large handle in the middle. As she does this, a large pillar of wood rises, along with a piece of fabric attached to it.

"We should be good to go in just a couple of minutes."

I look out at the water as she works. There is steam rising from it.

ANALYSIS

The water must be a higher temperature than average. There is a loud click and I look back over to Jasmine. The pillar now stands completely upright in the boat, approximately seventeen feet high.

Jasmine walks back over and lifts me up, along with the rest of the metal inside the cloth sack. She drops me into the boat, then pushes it towards the water. The boat slides quickly over the grass and splashes into the lake. Jasmine jumps into the back of the boat as we begin to move towards the island. I reach my hand out of the sack into the water.

TEMPERATURE – 90 DEGREES

"The temperature of this water is above average," I say.

"They tell me it's because there's thermal heat coming up from below the lake. Keeps everything warm all year round," Jasmine explains. There are no waves apart from the ones our ship is creating. There is a soft breeze that also fills the fabric attached to the pillar on the ship. This pulls us forward at a slow speed towards the island.

"I have never encountered such a phenomenon," I tell her.

We are over halfway to the island when I see more details of the area. The trees around the edges of the island are tall and thin, with large leaves. There also appear to be large spherical objects among the leaves.

SCANNING DATABASE – NO RESULTS

Beyond that, I can see more tall trees with thick vines growing up them. On this side of the water, there is also a small beach, but unlike the sand I have seen before, this is dark and black.

The boat slides gently onto the island.

"We're here," Jasmine says. The beach is covered in small black pebbles. The sun shines off of them to create a sparkling effect. I lean out of the boat and pick up a handful of the rocks.

"Is this beautiful?" I ask Jasmine. She looks at the small rocks in my hand and smiles.

"I guess they sort of are, but I've never really thought about it too much."

SUBROUTINE UPDATED – BEAUTY

Jasmine lifts me out of the boat and sets me up away from the water. She pulls the boat up onto the rocks and lowers the pole from the center. Once the pole is collapsed, she flips the boat back over, then lifts me and the cloth sack back up onto her shoulders.

We continue along a small path through the densely growing trees.

"These are not trees I have ever observed before," I tell her as we walk.

"Yeah, I guess you wouldn't have known all these where you were from," she says.

"Do you know the species here?" I ask.

"No, sorry. I know the ones on the beach back there are called palm trees. But most of these others I don't really know," she explains.

"Are the things growing here edible?" I ask.

"Oh yes! That I know." She points up to some of the trees. "Pretty much everything that grows here is completely edible," she explains. We continue through the trees until we come to a large clearing with a settlement.

"Is this your village?" I ask. She turns me around so I have a better view of the buildings.

"Yes! Welcome to St. Helens," she says. I can hear the excitement in her voice. I look around at the buildings here. Many appear to have been built from the same materials around the island. There are many buildings made from round green logs tied together with vines. The roofs are made from thickly-layered straw.

"These buildings are unlike any other structures I have encountered," I tell her. She turns back towards the houses, at the same time turning me away from them. "This is one of the larger settlements I have encountered." From the part I have observed, it is approximately twenty-seven percent bigger than Valentine.

"It's a good size for us. We have more settlements on the north coast too. But this is where I live," she says. "We should get you over to the forge."

She walks into the village. Many people are running around from building to building. There appear to be people from every age range. Elderly all the way to children. The people all wear lightweight fabric clothes with detailed patterning throughout. The same patterns can be seen decorating the buildings of the village as well.

Many of the villagers stare at us as we move through the center of the town. One person walks up to Jasmine.

"What's that?" they ask, pointing at me.

"Just some more scrap," Jasmine says. She sounds nervous.

"I would not define myself as scrap," I remind her.

"Quiet," she whispers to me.

"But it's tech. Just melt it down and be done with it," the person says.

"I'm bringing it to the forge now." Jasmine turns away from the person, but they continue to stare at me.

"Good, it really creeps me out," they say before walking away. Jasmine continues through the town, her pace faster than it previously had been. The other villagers continue to stare at us and she does not speak again.

Someone passes by, pulling a large cart filled with various fruits. I had observed these same fruits on the trees when we first arrived on this island. We pass by an open space between two buildings where a small garden is growing. I observe the people working as we pass them. They stop when they notice us.

"Have you ever seen a garden before?" Jasmine asks.

"Yes. My town has one," I tell her.

"What kind of stuff did they grow there?"

"They grow vegetables and herbs for the cafe," I say.

"That sounds really nice. Ours mostly grow herbs. Plus the fruits we gather from around the island."

"There are a number of natural resources here," I say. Jasmine pulls me away and we continue down the street. I have observed at least forty-six varieties of food in the time I have been here so far.

"The land here grows stuff really well. Something about the soil combined with the

heat makes it really easy to grow stuff."

"It is impressive that you have been able to disconnect entirely from the grid," I say.

"Well we were never really connected to it here."

"How are you able to survive?"

"Our families have lived here for generations. We've found a way to live in harmony with the land. Technology has never really factored into it for us," she says. I have never seen a village operate in this way. I was unaware humans were able to function without the use of electricity.

She leads us down the new path towards one of the larger buildings. There is an animal carved into the front and we enter through a hanging piece of cloth similar to the material of the sack Jasmine has me in.

The interior of the building is long and heavily decorated. The floor is a dark black dirt and there are large windows along the walls. Jasmine walks over to a doorway off of this large room and takes me inside. A man is sitting in front of a table.

"Hey, Pops," Jasmine says. The man turns around. He is wearing spectacles and his hair appears to be covered in the same black dirt as the floor.

"Is that Jasmine?" the man asks.

"Who else would it be?" She drops me onto the ground again, along with my bag, and the box with the holo-recorder falls onto the dirt floor. I look around the room and see the walls are covered with old pieces of technology.

"How long have you been away this time?" the man asks.

"Only a couple of days," Jasmine says.

"You bring me back any good scrap this time?"

"Not even going to ask how I'm doing?" She crosses her arms.

"Look, I'm busy. You have scrap or not?" Jasmine walks over and removes the cloth from around me. The man walks over.

"What is this?" he asks.

"My name is Bit," I say.

He does not look happy as he turns to Jasmine. "Why would you bring this here?"

"I thought we could help her out. She needs to do some repairs," Jasmine says. "Bit, this is my father, Elan."

"Her? Since when is it any more than scrap metal?"

"I would not define myself—"

Elan cuts me off. "You've melted down hundreds of androids, why is this one any different?" he says loudly.

"It just seems different," Jasmine replies.

"Why, because this one is still running?" He points to me. "It's not like it's actually alive or anything. It's scrap metal just like every other one." He leans down and looks me in the eyes.

"But what if you're wrong?" Jasmine says. Elan sighs and stands back up.

"Oh come on, Jas, your job is a scrapper. You find us metal and bring it back to be melted down. If you can't do that we'll just have to find something else for you."

Jasmine is quiet. I look around the room again and notice a large door at the back.

"That's what I thought. Plus if we don't get enough scrap we won't be able to help the northern settlement rebuild. We're already running behind on their order," he says.

"I may be able to assist you," I say.

He turns towards me. "What?"

"I require assistance to repair my legs. In return I will assist you with completing the work you need done."

"Look here, scrap,"—he turns away—"the most help you'll be is as building materi-al. We're just fine without your help."

"You know that's not true!" Jasmine rais-es her voice.

"What are you talking about?" Elan says.

"We've got too many settlements. Our supplies are getting stretched way too thin."

"Ridiculous. We're doing just fine."

"Do you know how far all the scrappers have to go to find parts these days?" Jasmine waves her arms around.

"You're just being an alarmist. Things are perfectly fine."

"Then you're completely blind." There is a pause after she says this.

"Leave." He points to the door we entered through.

"But—"

"We'll find another job for you. Clearly you're not cut out to be a scrapper anymore." I can see tears in Jasmine's eyes as she turns away from him.

She leans down to me. "I'm so sorry," she says before standing back up and walking out of the building. Elan turns to me next.

"Are you planning to melt me down?" I ask.

"Yes," he says.

"That will hinder my current objective," I explain. "I must find a way to restore power to the grid."

"Well then that's even more reason to make sure you don't go anywhere."

"I do not comprehend."

"Nothing good comes from having technology around. Our society is working just fine without it." He walks back over to his desk and sits down. I think about the people in Valentine.

"I do not believe that to be correct," I say.

"Oh really? This should be good."

"The power is utilized by villages other than yours. They require it to function," I say.

"My concern is for my village, not others."

"Do you not wish to help the other villages?"

"Why would I?"

QUERY UNKNOWN

SEARCHING DATABASE

"From my records I have encountered many humans who wish to help other people," I explain.

"Yeah, well not everyone is the same. I have to look out for the people I actually know. Why should I care about someone who I've never met?"

"I do not know," I say.

"Well consider it a final lesson in people, then." He walks over and lifts me onto his shoulders.

"Where are you taking me?" I ask.

"I'm gonna leave you in the forge. You'll be melted down first thing tomorrow." He walks with me towards the end of the room and pushes open the large door at the back. Beyond it is a glowing light.

ANALYISIS

My sensors read the high temperature. Elan drops me onto a flat metal table and walks back out of the room. The large door slams shut behind him.

I look around the room and observe more piles of old technology stacked up against the walls. There are a number of people working at different tables. Each person wears a red outfit that covers their entire body. Their faces are protected by thick black glass coverings. I look over to the first table.

ANALYSIS – LAPIN

There is a large engine sitting on the table from one of the LAPIN model cars. The person sitting at the table is slowly removing each piece of the engine and sorting them into small buckets. I watch for forty-three minutes as they work. Once a bucket has been filled it is brought over and added to one of the large piles of metal along the edge of the room.

In the center of the room is a large hole in the ground with an orange glow emanating from it. The people gather scraps of metal from one of the piles and dump them into a large container. The container is hooked onto a chain and five of them grab the edges, slowly dragging it towards the hole in the ground. As it is being dragged, others are digging patterns into the dirt next to the hole. One of the people walks up to me.

"What is the purpose of this room?" I ask. The person does not respond to me. "My name is Bit," I introduce myself. He writes notes on a piece of paper, which he then hangs on the side of the table.

"You're an android, aren't you?" he asks.

"That is correct," I tell him.

"Haven't ever seen a working android before." He walks away and I grab the paper. FOR DISASSEMBLY TOMORROW.

ANALYSIS

They must be planning to disassemble me into my components before melting me down. I look back to the other workers and the container is now suspended above the hole. After an hour and thirty-seven minutes, they use a series of sticks to push it towards the patterns in the dirt. They carefully turn the container over and the liquid metal flows out. It fills out the patterns and then the pot is slowly lowered to the ground.

In the distance, a bell rings. The people within the room all stop working and walk towards the exit. None look at me as they leave and the door closes loudly behind them. The only noise remaining is the sound coming from the glowing hole in the middle of the room.

CHAPTER EIGHT

OLIVIA

I pull myself off the table. My legs still do not function and I fall to the ground. I drag myself towards the door and attempt to open it, however the door will not move. I do not believe I should stay in this location if I wish to remain functioning.

I look around for another way out of the room, however the only exit appears to be the door I was brought in through. I turn back towards it and hear a faint noise coming from the other side. Then a loud crash and the door swings open. It is another one of the workers, but their outfit seems baggy and ill-fitting. They grab me and pull me up onto their shoulders. Then they walk into the next room and place me into a chair.

"For what purpose have you moved me?" I ask. The figure removes the dark glass from their face and I recognize Jasmine.

"Hey, Bit, I'm here to get you out."

"You have returned."

"My dad would kill me if he knew I was here," she says as she removes the rest of the red suit from over her clothing. "Will you be able to walk?"

"My legs are still inoperable," I say as I sit up.

"What do you need to fix them?"

"I will require my bag of supplies." She looks over to the pile of scraps she had brought in with me earlier. The bag is still there and she runs over to grab it.

"Here you go." She hands it to me and I remove the repair kit. I open the panel on my left leg and examine the circuits.

"How's it look?" Jasmine asks.

"The circuits are burned out," I tell her. "They will need to be replaced."

"Well I'm sure there must be something in here we can use. There's a bunch of old scrap," Jasmine says. I look around the room.

ANALYSIS

"There is a radio on the opposite wall." I point at the small radio and she grabs it from the pile of other technology. I take it from her and open the back.

MAINTENANCE MODE STARTED

I remove the circuit from the radio.

"Will you be able to use that?" Jasmine asks.

"Yes, this part will be compatible with my legs," I inform her. I remove the old circuit from my leg and toss it aside. "Thank you for assisting me."

"I just don't agree with melting you down. It feels wrong."

"For what reason?" I pull out my welding arc and begin to fuse the new circuit back into my leg.

"Well you're, like, alive!"

"That is incorrect. I am not alive," I tell her.

"But it feels like you are. I mean, we have conversations. You ask questions. It doesn't feel like you're just a machine."

I finish attaching the circuit back into my leg and close the panel.

REBOOT PROCESS ACTIVATED

My leg moves around.

"Oh, it worked!"

"I must now mend the other leg," I inform her, opening the panel on my other leg.

ANALYSIS

The artificial muscle is entirely burned out. There are many sections that have been melted together.

"That looks bad," Jasmine says as she examines my leg. I look around the room.

"I require anything with a screen," I say. Jasmine gets up and begins picking more items off the walls and bringing them to me. I remove the front of a small device with a screen and peel off the mesh that sits underneath the glass. Jasmine continues to stack a small pile of devices next to me.

"Will these really work?" she asks. I detach the artificial muscles from inside my leg. The main section has been entirely burned out.

"It will not be an ideal fix. I will require the correct parts as soon as possible." I work quickly to cover the burned area with the pieces of metal mesh, softly hammering them into shape.

"What're you doing?" Jasmine asks.

"This mesh will help conduct electricity along the leg again," I explain.

"Isn't that what all the wires are for?"

"The wires are for the sensors along my leg. The main source of electricity into my foot is through the artificial muscle," I explain. After another couple of minutes, the mesh is fully fit into the hole of my artificial muscle.

"Is it fixed?"

SYSTEM REBOOT ENGAGED

The muscle glows red as electricity begins to flow through it again. I attempt to move my leg. It responds quickly.

DIAGNOSTIC MODE STARTED – HARDWARE AT 86% INTEGRITY

"My leg appears to be eighty-six percent functional now," I say.

MAINTENANCE MODE ENDED

"Will you be able to move like that?"

I close the panel on my leg and stand up. "Yes. I appear to be functional enough to walk again." I place my toolkit back into the bag and look across the room for the holo-recorder box laying on the floor. I walk over and pick it up. My legs feel unbalanced.

"That was in your bag before, wasn't it?" Jasmine asks.

"That is correct."

"What kind of tool is it?"

"That is not a tool," I inform her. "It is a device called a holo-recorder."

"A holo-recorder? What does that do?"

I open the lid and remove the device. "This allows a person to record an image of a person or events," I say.

Jasmine grabs one of the discs from the box. "And what're these?"

"Those are recordings. They can be placed into the holo-recorder and played back."

She hands me the disc. "Can you show me one?"

"Yes." I open the holo-recorder and put the disc inside, then press the power button. The holo-recorder turns on and the image of Ava appears.

"That's incredible!" Jasmine exclaims. She looks around the recording, observing the image of Ava closely.

"This technology is outdated," I inform her.

"Well it's all new to me!"

QUERY

"Do you not collect technology?" I ask.

"Yeah, but none of it actually works! I don't think I've ever seen something like this in my life."

I press the button on the holo-recorder and the recording begins.

"Hello, my darling!"

"Whose voice is that?" Jasmine asks.

"That is the voice of Olivia. She is the one who made these recordings," I say.

"What's it today?" Ava responds to Olivia.

"We're going on an adventure today!" Olivia says. The figure of Ava rolls her eyes.

"Oh, are we really?" Ava asks.

Jasmine runs her hand through the recording. "Incredible."

"Yes! I've found a secret hatch north of the town!" Olivia exclaims.

"And what, we're just going to go explore it?" Ava asks.

"Of course. I didn't even tell you the best part yet!"

"Oh, and what's that?" Ava asks.

I press stop on the holo-recording. Jasmine seems to have an understanding of its functionality now.

"Wait a second! You can't just stop it there!"

"Do you not have an understanding of how the holo-recorder functions? I can attempt to explain it again if that would help you understand," I offer.

"What, no! I get how it works."

"Then I do not understand why you do not wish to stop viewing," I say.

"I want to see what happens next!"

"For what purpose?"

"I have to know what happens! I've never seen other people recorded like this," she says.

I do not fully understand her reasoning, but I press the button again and the recording starts back up. Ava reappears.

"Oh, and what's that?" Ava says.

"It's apparently from before the flooding!" Olivia's voice says.

Ava stops smiling. *"What do you mean?"*

"I found the entrance buried in the snow, but apparently it was all abandoned before the flooding happened," Olivia says.

"Wait, but how would you know that?"

"There was a seal from when it was closed. The date was hundreds of years ago."

"There's no way a place like that is safe," Ava says.

"Oh come on, if it was safe where would the fun be?"

"And did you tell your dad about it?" Ava asks. There is a pause.

"Not yet..." Olivia responds.

"You always find the most creative ways to get us into trouble."

"You know you love it," Olivia says.

"Well, give me that," Ava says as she reaches out towards the recording. The camera motion becomes blurred. *"If you're going to make us do this I want it on record that it was your idea, ok?"* The image turns around and the figure of Olivia appears completely out of focus.

"Fine," Olivia's voice starts. *"My name is Olivia, and tomorrow this chicken and I are going to explore someplace super cool,"* she says.

Jasmine squints her eyes. "It's all out of focus."

"Wait, hold on," Ava says.

"What's up?" Olivia asks.

"It's not in focus, give me a sec," Ava says. The camera shakes around before the image comes into focus on Olivia.

"You good? My name is Olivia and to-morrow—" I press the pause button, cutting off Olivia's voice.

FACIAL RECOGNITION STARTED

"Wait, what's going on?" Jasmine asks.

"I do not know," I say.

"But her face…" Jasmine starts. "She's you."

FACIAL RECOGNITION COMPLETE – 100% MATCH

The image staring at me from the holo-recorder is my own face.

"I don't understand," says Jasmine.

"I do not understand either."

"Is that you?"

SCANNING MEMORY – NO RESULTS

"I have no recorded memory of that event," I tell her.

"But if it's not you then why do you look exactly the same?" Jasmine asks.

"I do not know." My brain is working to try and process this information.

"When were those recordings from?"

"They were recorded approximately one-hundred-and-eight years ago."

"Well, that's insane. How many of them are there?"

"There are one-hundred-and-thirty-one recordings in total."

"And how many have you watched?"

"I have watched twelve recordings," I tell her.

"Why only twelve?" She starts looking through all the other discs in the box.

"I obtained the relevant information I required."

"Relevant information? And what was that?"

"There is information in one of these discs regarding a power system. I am attempting to find further information regarding this power system by locating the origin of these recordings," I explain.

"But what about Olivia? Why do you look like her?" Jasmine asks.

"I do not have any further information about that."

"I mean, look at that, even your eyes look exactly the same!"

ANALYSIS

"There is a one-hundred percent match between our features."

"See, what does that mean?"

"I do not have sufficient data to determine that."

"But it's your recordings! How can you not know?" she asks loudly.

"It does not appear to be a coincidence," I say. "The probability of that happening is extremely low." Before Jasmine can respond, I hear voices from outside. I press the power button on the holo-recorder and the image disappears.

"Damn it, we were way too loud. Someone's coming to check on the building," Jasmine says. "We have to go right now." She pulls me towards one of the windows of the building and quickly climbs out, then helps pull me through. My leg is not in optimal condition for climbing, but we manage to get through the window.

"Stay down," Jasmine says.

EYESIGHT ADJUSTING

I hide below the window. The door to the building opens and a number of voices enter the room we had just been in. Jasmine attempts to make herself as quiet as possible. I remain motionless next to her. The voices start to fade.

"That was way too close," she says.

"For what reason are we hiding?"

"Well, if they find out that I took you I'll be in huge trouble. Taking supplies is a punishable offense," she explains.

"What supplies have you taken?"

"I took you!"

"I am not supplies," I inform her.

"Look, I know that. But that's not how they see it." She looks around us quickly. "To them you're just more metal to be melted down and used for building materials for our new settlements. That's why we've got to get you out of here."

"I do not comprehend why Elan does not wish to assist other communities," I say.

"That's just how people are sometimes, Bit. Not everyone's nice."

"I have encountered people that did not like me before," I say.

"Really?"

"Yes. However those people would still help other humans whenever given the chance. They did not like me because I was not one of them," I say.

"I'm sorry to hear that." Jasmine looks around the corner of the building. "Let's go." She pulls my arm and we quickly run to the other side of the street. We step off the road into the line of trees. There are small fires lit along the edge of the street that had not been there previously.

ACCESSING COMPASS

We are moving away from the side of the island that we arrived on.

"For what reason are we not returning to the location we arrived at?" I ask. We continue deeper into the trees away from the street.

EYESIGHT ADJUSTING

"The wind around the island only blows north. We have to use the other set of boats to get off the island," she explains as we run.

Despite the darkness, Jasmine does not appear to require guidance to move through the trees on the island. We slowly descend until we reach the shore. There is an identical boat to the one we arrived in.

"Get in," Jasmine says. I step into the boat and she quickly pushes it into the water, jumping in afterwards.

"Are you not going to raise the sail of the boat?" I ask.

"There's no time. The boat will be the first place they look for me." I look back to the island and see lights moving through the trees. The boat continues to drift away from the shore. Jasmine places her hand on my back and pushes me down.

"For what—" I start to ask. She covers my mouth with her hand as she crouches down next to me. She points back towards the land. I see a group of people emerge from the trees onto the shore holding lanterns and looking around. I am unable to hear them from our distance.

The lights of their lanterns move around the edge of the island until they are no longer in sight.

"It looks like they've moved off," Jasmine says quietly. The boat continues to drift slowly across the water towards the northern shore of the lake.

After two hours, the boat arrives at the opposite shore. Jasmine climbs out and pulls the boat onto the grass. I step out onto land.

"Let's keep going. We can probably make it up to the Northern Tunnel before the sun comes up," she says.

SEARCHING DATABASE – NO RESULTS

"I have no information about the Northern Tunnel," I tell her.

"Wait, really? How were you navigating before I met you?" She pulls the boat fully up onto the grass.

"I have recorded a number of maps of the coastline that I am following," I explain.

"Yeah, but when're those from?" We walk away from the shore.

"They are from approximately sixty-two years before the flooding."

"Oh, no wonder! Those are way out of date!"

"I was not aware of this."

"Yeah, they carved a giant tunnel through the mountains. No one's touched it in ages, but it should still be there." She points towards the large mountains ahead of us.

"That will be a more efficient route of travel."

"You're telling me!" she says. "Were you just going to try to walk over the mountains?"

"That is correct."

"Well, then it's a good thing you've got me along. It's only about two hours from here."

We continue north from the lake. The trees in this area are no longer of the variety growing in St. Helens. They are large pine trees of the same variety I have seen in this region. They must be more adaptable to the climate in this area. I do not recall trees such as this growing in Valentine.

The path to the mountain is overgrown with thick moss and does not appear to have been walked on recently. I look behind us and see the indentations on the moss from where I had stepped. Jasmine, however, does not sink into it the same way.

"What's up?" I turn forward and see Jasmine looking back at me.

"I was observing the ground," I inform her.

"Well there's plenty of time for that later." She continues to walk ahead of me. After three hours, we arrive at the base of the mountain. There is a large door in front of us, approximately the same height as the tree line.

"Here we are. This is the entrance to the Northern Tunnel," Jasmine says.

"Is there a mechanism for opening the door?" I ask.

"Oh yeah, I think there was some kind of panel to open it." She looks around. "Ah, there it is!" She runs over to a large metal box next to the door and opens it. I walk up next to her. The inside of the box has numerous wires that have been burned and melted together.

ANALYSIS
The wires resemble the lanterns from
Valentine after the festival.

"It doesn't look like any of it's working."

"The mechanism is no longer connected
to the grid system," I inform her.

"What do you mean?"

"When the grid went offline this mechanism was likely rendered inoperable," I explain.

"But is there any way we can get enough
power to open the door?"

SYSTEM PROCESSING

"I am running simulations," I tell her.

SIMULATION ENDED

"It would appear that my system may
have enough power to open the door," I say.

"Wait, really? And that won't affect
you?"

"That is correct." I walk over to the box,
locate the power conduit to the door and find
the appropriate wire. I open the panel on my
chest where my battery is located.

"What's that?"

"That is my power source," I tell her.

She continues to stare at it. "Yeah, but
why's it doing that?"

"I do not understand what you mean."

"Why's it glowing red like that?"

"That is how I am built," I inform her.
My power source has always produced this

glow. The red light illuminates the box in front of us.

EYESIGHT ADJUSTING

I grab the wires from the conduit and hold them against my battery. There is a soft humming noise as the power surges through my wires. Next to us there is a loud crashing noise.

HARDWARE AT 85% INTEGRITY

"What was that?" Jasmine asks. I remove the wires from my battery and close the panel on my chest again.

"I used my power source to jump-start the opening mechanism of the door," I explain.

"I can't believe that worked," she says.

"I already informed you that it would be possible." The door slowly begins to swing open and I close the box.

"Well, then I guess we can keep on moving." Jasmine steps into the tunnel and I follow. My leg creaks slightly as I put weight onto it.

The interior of the tunnel is constructed from concrete and has large circular holes in the ceiling above us. Each of the holes has a thick glass covering and I can see the sky beyond. Jasmine and I walk along the tunnel. White and yellow lines are painted along the smooth black floor.

SEARCHING DATABASE – NO RESULT

My database shows no record of the meaning of these stripes.

"You know, I don't even know how long this tunnel is."

"I do not have that information either," I inform her.

"I'm sure we'll be fine. We just have to keep walking, right?"

"That is correct," I say. I see an object in the distance ahead of us and we walk towards it.

SCAN STARTED

"What's that?" Jasmine says. Her vision did not pick it up until minutes after mine.

SCAN ENDED

DATABASE MATCH – CAR

"The object appears to be a car," I inform her.

"A car?"

"That is correct."

"What's a car?"

"A method of transportation," I inform her.

She walks over to the car and opens one of the doors. "How does it work?" She climbs inside.

"The cars of that era used a fuel source called gasoline to power an engine," I explain.

"You think this thing still runs?"

"I do not," I say. She begins pressing the buttons on the dashboard of the car. It does not respond.

"Looks like you called it." She closes the door and we continue down the tunnel. We pass by a number of other cars that are stopped on the road. They do not appear to have been in use for many years. However, unlike the ones around Valentine, these cars are not rusted or falling apart. My hypothesis is that being closed off has preserved the contents of the tunnel.

"You know, these would've made good scrap." Jasmine looks at all of the cars as we pass them.

"Perhaps you will still be able to utilize them as scrap."

"Yeah, maybe when I head back. If they'll have me again someday." She stops walking.

"For what reason have you stopped?" I ask. She points over to the side of the tunnel. There is a large open space with a building inside. Above the building, the words REST STOP are carved into the concrete.

"I wanna check that place out," she says.

"For what purpose?"

"I need a bit of a rest. We've been walking for hours now." She starts towards the open area. "And who knows, there might be some supplies in there that we could use."

"I will assist you in looking for supplies," I tell her. We pass under the sign into the large open space beyond it. The ceiling has the same holes in the roof. The room is tall and there are concrete columns stretching the length of the building. Jasmine walks over to a small table surrounded by chairs and sits down.

"I will begin searching for supplies," I inform her.

"Yeah, I'm just gonna rest my eyes for a sec." She closes her eyes as I walk around the building. There are a number of small entrances off of the main room, each leading to a different kind of room. One of them is filled with assorted clothing. I grab clothes from one of the piles and put them into a bag that is hanging nearby. I move onto the next room.

This one is filled with a variety of old technology. There are screens around the room, however none of them appear to be active. I continue along to the next room which is filled with a variety of food products. Many of these are expired and no longer fit for human consumption. I look through the racks of food until I find a shelf filled with metal cans. These appear to be sealed completely. Theoretically, the contents should be preserved as well. I place a number of the cans into the bag alongside the clothes.

I continue to explore the various rooms throughout this building. All of them appear to have been completely abandoned for a number of years. This seems to have been a gathering location for travelers passing through the tunnel. I come to one room with a series of maps along the walls. I pick up a map and examine it. The details are vastly different than the ones stored in my memory.

SCAN STARTED

Despite these maps being more current, they are still not fully accurate to the current terrain. The coastlines in these maps do not reflect the flooding. This map shows a larger landmass that no longer exists above sea level. I place the map back onto the rack where I had retrieved it from.

DATABASE UPDATED – GEOGRA-PHY

I exit into the main room and walk over to the table where Jasmine is sleeping. I sit down on the opposite side of the table. I let her sleep while I examine the details of the map in my memory. This tunnel appears to end at the exit to the city of June.

Jasmine wakes up.

"How long was I out?" she asks.

"You were asleep for approximately three hours and twenty-seven minutes," I inform her. She looks up through the holes in the ceiling.

"Looks like the sun's coming up. We should probably get going." She gets up from the table. "What's that you've got there?" She points at the bag of supplies I have picked up.

"I have found supplies for you in these rooms," I tell her.

"For me?"

"That is correct. I do not require such supplies."

"That's really nice of you, Bit. Come on, let's head back to the road." She picks up the bag and we walk together onto the road, continuing north through the tunnel. The sun is now shining through the roof. There are more cars stopped along the road as we walk. They do not appear to be in disrepair, however it would take a more in-depth examination to determine their exact condition.

"It's much easier to see with all the light in here," Jasmine says.

"My eyesight is capable of adjusting to any lighting environment," I inform her. She smiles.

"Well, at least it's easier for me." We continue past the other cars in the tunnel. I have recorded 271 vehicles in the tunnel so far. Jasmine does not speak for another two hours.

"How old are you?" Jasmine asks.

"I have been operational for ninety-one years."

"Wait, really?"

"That is correct."

"I can't even imagine what you've experienced." She looks up through the ceiling.

"I have a full recorded database with my memories."

"Really? You've never forgotten anything?" She looks back down.

"I am incapable of forgetting anything," I tell her.

"Well I guess that's nice, in a way."

"In what way is that nice?"

"Well, even years later all those people you've met kind of live on through you, right?"

"I do not comprehend."

"I mean, like, even though they passed away, you still remember them." She stops walking. "So, like, a part of those people is still around." I do not fully comprehend this but Jasmine resumes walking and I continue alongside her. After another ten hours, I see a large opening ahead of us. There is a strong breeze coming from it and a bright white light.

"You think that's the end of the tunnel?" Jasmine asks as she notices the same light.

"I do." That is the most logical explanation. As we get closer, there is a row of cars blocking our path. Jasmine climbs up onto one of them. I attempt to climb up after her.

HARDWARE ERROR

The response in my leg is delayed and I am unable to fully climb onto the car. Jasmine reaches down her hand.

"Lemme help you up." I grab her hand and she pulls me onto the car. We climb down the other side and the two of us walk towards the end of the tunnel.

EYESIGHT ADJUSTING

I am able to see the tunnel door, which is opened slightly. The temperature near this door is significantly lower than the rest of the tunnel.

"It's freezing here," Jasmine says. We reach the door and step through the opening.

EYESIGHT ADJUSTING

My eyes take longer to adjust to the light surrounding us. The landscape is a bright white.

We are standing on top of a steep hillside that is entirely white and cold. In front of us stretches a large city with a number of wooden buildings built into the side of a steep cliff. Beyond the city is a large, flat landscape with a single large hill and a white powder floating through the air.

ANALYSIS COMPLETE

MATERIAL IDENTIFIED – SNOW

At the edge of the flat landscape is a tall building sitting on a cliffside.

"Look at that," Jasmine says. I look over at her and she is pointing at a large wooden sign next to the tunnel. The sign is heavily worn but still reads, WELCOME TO JUNE.

CHAPTER NINE

JUNE

"So I guess this is June," Jasmine says. I examine the wooden sign. There are a number of letters missing from the end and it is covered with a thick layer of ice. I walk forward and the ground cracks underneath my feet. I look down to examine the ground further. My feet have crushed a thin sheet of ice.

"Be cautious while walking," I tell Jasmine. I look over to her and she is going through the bag of supplies. "Is there something you require?" I ask.

"Yeah I need something more to wear."

"For what purpose?"

"It's way too cold here, Bit. I'm used to the warmer weather." She pulls out a large piece of fabric from the bag and wraps it around herself, covering her entire body. I recognize the item as a shawl; it is a thick material and has an intricate pattern woven through the fibers. Jasmine raises the hood of the shawl over her head.

"Will that be adequate?" I ask.

"I should be good now, but we should try to find someplace inside soon," Jasmine says.

We walk forward and at the edge, there are a series of stone steps built into the hill. Jasmine and I walk down these stairs towards the city. Along the sides of the path, there are large pillars of wood with figures carved into them. Similar to the welcome sign, they are coated in a thick layer of ice which does not allow me to determine the exact details of the posts. Jasmine stops to look at one of the pillars.

"It's kind of beautiful, isn't it?"

"In what way is it beautiful?" I ask.

"I don't really know, guess it just reminds me of the carvings we had back in St. Helens." She continues walking down the stairs. I examine the carved wooden pillar again.

SUBROUTINE UPDATED – BEAUTY

The stairs end at a stone street through the city. Along the sides of the street are large buildings that appear to be constructed from thick tree logs.

ANALYSIS COMPLETE

There is a high probability that they have been constructed from the same red trees we encountered in the forests south of here due to the same coloration and average size of each log. Jasmine stops again and looks out beyond the city.

"It's like the snow stretches forever." She points beyond the buildings. "Like, even there it's just completely flat for as far as I can see."

"The temperature here must allow for snow the entire year."

Jasmine nods and we continue walking. There are many buildings lining the street.

"Let's try there." She points at a building in the distance. There is a light pouring out from inside, and many people from the city going in and out. They wear thick fabric coverings similar to the one Jasmine now wears.

We enter the building through the large hanging fabric at the entrance. There are dozens of people sitting at tables with food and drinks. At the far side of the room is a large stone hearth with a fire inside. I can feel the heat radiating from it. Jasmine walks over to a large table and sits down with some of the people there.

"Hello," she says. I walk over and sit down beside her.

"Never seen you two before. You from around here?" one of the people asks.

"Nope, we just got here. We're coming from St. Helens," Jasmine tells him.

"Wow, that's pretty far off! Don't get too many people around here. Not an easy trip after all," he says as he takes a drink from a large mug. "I'm Halvar."

"I'm Jasmine, and this is Bit." She points to me.

"Aren't you getting cold?" Halvar asks me.

"I am not. My body is capable of regulating temperature on its own," I inform him.

"Is that so?"

"That is correct," I answer.

"Hey, Halvar, do you know anywhere in town where we'd be able to stay for the night?" Jasmine asks.

"Indeed I do. There is an inn across the town which is open to any who need it."

"We require directions," I tell him.

"It's simple, you're on the right level already so all you have to do is follow this street along until you see the building with a large shell sign in front of it," he says.

"What do you mean 'right level'?" Jasmine asks.

"Oh that's right, you guys probably don't know yet. So because the whole city is built into a hill, all the streets are on different levels," he says.

"How do you get between them?" Jasmine asks.

"Every couple of buildings there are stone steps that connect the levels. So right now we're on level fourteen and it goes down until you reach the seafront," he explains.

"I did not observe any body of water in this area," I tell him.

"Just because you didn't see it don't mean it's not there."

"So where is it?" Jasmine asks.

"Did you see that flat area at the bottom of the city?"

"Yes," I say.

"That's it."

"What do you mean?" Jasmine asks.

"Centuries ago that used to be the ocean. But when the flooding happened everything up this way froze," he says.

"So that's…" Jasmine starts to say.

"The frozen ocean," he finishes.

"I can't believe that."

"Eh, none of us have ever seen anything different. It's just how it is. Kind of weird, and beautiful too," Halvar says.

SUBROUTINE UPDATED – BEAUTY

"It's just so foreign to me," Jasmine says.

"Yeah, but most things are if you've never seen 'em before," Halvar says.

"I guess that's true. Thank you so much for all your help," Jasmine says. She gets up from the table.

"There's no need for you all to go just yet." Halvar places a bowl of food onto the table. "Let's get you two something warm to drink."

"Are you sure?" Jasmine asks.

"Of course I'm sure! My family and I have run this tavern for generations and we're always here to take in strays," he says.

QUERY – STRAYS

"What is the definition of 'strays'?" I ask. Halvar laughs.

"It just means you two look a little lost," he says. "I'll be back in a sec with those drinks." He walks to the long table at the back of the room.

DATABASE UPDATED – STRAYS

Jasmine pulls her shawl closer. She does not speak until Halvar returns with two large mugs.

"Thank you," she says as he places them on the table. Steam rises from the liquid inside.

"Not a problem. You two enjoy now." He walks away and Jasmine quietly drinks the liquid. She does not look up.

"You know, I didn't even say goodbye before I left," she says.

"To whom did you not say goodbye?"

"My whole family. I just snuck out and left." She takes another drink from the mug in front of her.

"You did not appear to be on good terms with your father," I remind her.

"I'm not. But I didn't even tell my mom. And now I doubt I'd ever be allowed to come back."

"For what reason would you not be allowed to return?" I ask.

"I broke the law. They'd banish me anyways."

"Then the outcome is the same no matter the action."

"Yeah, but I think it's only just hitting me that I don't have a home to go back to anymore." She puts the mug down on the table.

"You may accompany me back to Valentine," I tell her.

"Wait, really?" She looks up at me.

"Yes. Once we have located the power source I will return it to Valentine," I explain.

"Are you sure they'd even want me there?"

"There have been a number of other people who have moved to Valentine from other locations. I do not foresee you moving there being any different."

Jasmine smiles. "Hmmm. Valentine, huh?" She grabs some of the food in front of her and starts eating. I look around the room. There are a number of people seated at every table. Most wear thick clothing similar to the shawl Jasmine is wearing. I watch as Halvar brings food and drinks to everyone. Jasmine finishes her meal.

"Well, we should probably find that place Halvar told us about." Jasmine gets up from the table and I follow her. Halvar waves to us and I wave back as we walk out onto the street. The sun has gone down further in the sky. Along the street, large fires are being lit. The light from these fires illuminate the streets.

Jasmine and I continue down the stone road, in the opposite the direction we had come from. I observe the buildings as we walk. Many have elaborate decorations carved into the wood. After a few minutes of walking, we arrive at a large building with a scallop shell carved into it.

"I believe this is the location Halvar directed us to," I say to Jasmine. She looks up from under her hood.

"Let's get inside quick. It's freezing out here." She quickly runs inside.

The interior is small with a desk at the back of the room and a person standing behind it. On either side of the desk are wooden staircases. One staircase leads up and the other leads down. There is a large fireplace similar to the one in the previous building that provides light throughout the room.

Jasmine walks up to the woman at the front desk.

"Hey, there! What brings you two out this way?" the woman asks. She appears surprised to see us.

"We are looking for information regarding someone who used to live here," I tell her.

"Oh really?"

"That is correct," I say.

"Well, first off, we're actually looking for someplace to stay for the night. Halvar over at the tavern sent us," Jasmine interrupts.

"Well, any friend of Halvar is welcome here," she says.

"Thank you," Jasmine says. The woman grabs a small candle off of the table and leads us up one of the wooden staircases.

"And if you head back his way you be sure to tell him to swing by and say hello in person." We arrive on the second floor of the building which has a series of doors along a long hallway. The woman opens one of the doors and beckons us inside.

"You two can stay in here for the night. If you need anything, I'll be downstairs." She closes the door behind us. There are two small beds in the room. Jasmine walks over to the first bed and lays down. This room also has a large stone hearth with a fire burning in it. The light and heat from the fire fill the room.

"It'll be nice to sleep in a real bed again," Jasmine says.

"I do not require sleep," I remind her. She laughs.

"Then it'll be nice for me," she says. I sit down on the other bed. "I feel like we've just been going non-stop."

I set down my bag and take out the holo-recorder box and parcel from Bruce. Jasmine reaches over and picks up the parcel.

"You know, I've been meaning to ask, what is this?"

"That was given to me by the mayor of Valentine before I left," I tell her.

"So what is it? You had it back when I first picked you up."

"It is a gift," I explain.

"Yeah I know that! But what's inside?"

"I do not know," I say.

"Well why don't you open it?" she asks as she hands me the wrapped item. I pull on the twine and the knot comes undone. I un-wrap the colorful fabric and find a small fig-ure. It is carved from a white stone and re-sembles the statue that stands in the fountain in Valentine.

"It's beautiful," Jasmine says.

SUBROUTINE UPDATED – BEAUTY

"It is the same statue as the one located in Valentine," I say.

"Oh, really? That's sweet of them to give that to you." I place the carved figure onto the bed and pick up the holo-recorder.

"You gonna watch another one of those?"

"I am."

"You think there's more info on one of those about where we need to go?"

"I am hopeful."

"Hopeful?" she asks.

"Yes, there is a particular outcome which I desire," I tell her.

"Sorry, I just don't think I've ever heard you express an emotion like that," she says.

"I do not have emotions," I remind her.

"But what about hope?"

SYSTEM PROCESSING – NO RE-SULTS.

"I do not have sufficient data to analyze that."

She laughs quietly. "It's just a very human thing to feel," she says. I open the holo-recorder box and remove the discs. I put aside the ones we have already viewed, open the holo-recorder and place a new disc inside. I press the power button and it turns on. An image of a street in June appears in front of us. The light from the holo-recorder fills the room, obscuring the light from the fireplace.

"So we got in a bit of trouble last week," the recording says. I recognize Olivia's voice again. She appears to be walking down the street, however the camera is recording in the opposite direction from her.

"We found this cool, abandoned place and went out to explore it." There is a pause in the recording. *"But some stuff happened that wasn't too great. I don't want to get into all that right now."* Her voice sounds different.

"She sounds sad," Jasmine says. She is staring closely at the recording.

"I told my dad about what we found and he kind of freaked out. He says I'm not allowed to see Ava anymore," Olivia says. The recording turns and walks down a set of the stone steps we had seen between the levels of June.

"I'm still going to, obviously. But something about the place we went really freaked dad out," Olivia says. The recording turns onto one of the streets. She walks towards a tall building at the end of the road.

"Hey, I remember that building," says Jasmine.

"I also recall that location," I tell her.

"It's at the end of that cliff I think." The recording approaches the building; it is large and octagonal with a dome on top.

"I think he was talking about moving his lab up there," Olivia says. The recording passes through the entrance to the building. *"So I think I might take this place over once he moves all this crap out of here,"* she says.

The recording spins around showing a cluttered room full of books before stopping.

"So she used to go there?" Jasmine asks.

"That would appear to be accurate."

"I wonder what that place is."

"From the items inside, my hypothesis is that it is a library," I say.

"Oh, really? You think that's where we need to go?"

"I believe it may contain information that we require."

"Well we should check it out."

"I shall gather my bag."

She grabs my arm. "No, Bit, not right now. I meant like tomorrow morning."

"For what purpose do you desire to wait?"

"We've done a lot of traveling. I need a little rest before we explore any more," she says.

"Very well. We shall depart tomorrow." I remove the disc from the holo-recorder and place the next one into it. Ava appears on the recording.

"So care to tell us where we are, Ava?" Olivia's voice asks.

"We're somewhere where we're not supposed to be," Ava says.

"Oh come on, I thought we had found your sense of adventure," Olivia says.

"Nope, you just dragged me along again." The camera moves and the recording shows a large door in the ground.

"Well let's go!" Olivia says. Ava reaches down to the door and pulls a large lever. The door on the ground swings upwards and the camera moves closer.

"It's open," Ava says. She looks inside the hole. *"And it looks like there's a staircase,"* she continues. The camera zooms in on the hole and shows a small spiral staircase within.

"Well, ladies first," Olivia's voice says.

"You're a lady too!"

"Yeah, but I'm also holding the camera. You can't expect me to go down first!"

"That's such a cop-out," Ava says. Despite this, she begins to climb down the staircase. Olivia follows her with the recorder and they descend into the ground. As they do, the recording cuts out. I turn off the holo-recorder and place it back into the box along with the discs.

"There's so much we still don't know about what happened with them," Jasmine says.

"That is correct."

"Like what did they find down there?"

"I do not know."

"Well hopefully we can find some answers tomorrow," Jasmine says. "Goodnight, Bit." She closes her eyes.

"Goodnight," I tell her, then lay down on my bed.

ENTERING SLEEP MODE

SLEEP MODE ENDED
I sit up from the bed.

"Well, it's about time! I thought you'd never be up!" Jasmine says. She is standing next to my bed.

"I was in my sleep mode," I tell her.

"Clearly! But I've been up for hours." There is sun shining in from the window across the room.

"For what purpose were you up so early?"

"I couldn't sleep. Way too excited about finally getting some answers." I notice she is carrying my bag on her shoulder.

"You are holding my bag."

"Yeah! I wanted to be sure you were ready to go." She hands me the bag and I place it over my shoulder. "You ready now?"

"I am ready," I tell her. She moves quickly to the door, opens it, and is in the hallway within seconds. I follow her out and we walk down the wooden staircase into the main room of the house. The woman who had been at the desk last night is no longer there. We walk outside.

EYESIGHT ADJUSTING

"It's over there," Jasmine says, pointing to the other side of the city. I look over to the large building. It appears similar to the recording in the holo-recorder, however some of the features have been altered since the recording was created. We continue along the street past the inn. There are dozens of people out. Many of them turn to stare at me as we walk.

"We will have to move to a lower level of the city in order to reach the building," I determine after observing the streets.

"Well, let's go down here," Jasmine says, walking down a series of stone steps. These steps also have large wooden poles alongside them with figures carved into the wood. We reach the next level down and continue until we have descended three more times.

"This is the correct level," I inform Jasmine. She stops walking.

"Oh yeah?" she asks. She looks around and sees the tower above the other buildings. "Yeah, there it is."

As we approach it, it becomes clear that the building has aged significantly since the time of the holo-recording. We arrive at the entrance. Unlike the other buildings in the town, this one is constructed from white stone. There is a sign carved into the stone above the door which reads, WARDEN-CLYFFE LIGHTHOUSE.

QUERY – WARDENCLYFFE

ERROR – FILE NOT FOUND

This building also has a metal door instead of the fabric hangings that all of the wooden buildings have.

"Should we go inside?" Jasmine asks.

"Yes," I respond. I grab the handle on the door and pull it open. We step inside and find a small octagonal room. In the center is a metal spiral staircase that leads up through the ceiling. There is a woman on the other side of the room who greets us.

"Hey there! I'm Runa," she says. She reaches out her hand to Jasmine who shakes it. She then reaches her hand out to me and I mimic what Jasmine had just done.

"Hey, I'm Jasmine and this is Bit," Jasmine says. "Is it ok for us to be here?"

"Of course! This is a public building. Plus, not too many people want to come here anyway," Runa says.

"For what reason?" I ask.

"Well, there's just not too much here anymore," Runa says.

"What about all this?" Jasmine asks, pointing around the room. There are desks and bookcases along the walls.

"Oh, most of this is just the town archives now," Runa explains. "Is there something you wanted to look up?"

"Yes, we're trying to find information about an inventor who used to live up here," Jasmine says. I notice something on one of the desks. I walk over and pick up a framed photograph. There is a man standing next to a figure who looks exactly like me.

"Who are the people in this photograph?" I ask. Runa walks over and takes the photograph out of my hands to study it. She stares at it closely before looking back at me. She examines me, then looks back at the photograph.

"Well, I could swear that this one's you," Runa says, "but that would be completely impossible."

"Why's that?" Jasmine asks.

"Because both of these people have been dead for ages," Runa says. "This photograph is from almost a century ago."

"That makes sense," Jasmine says.

"Then how is she standing here?" Runa points at me.

"I am an android," I tell her.

"But why do you look exactly like her?"

"I do not know."

"We were hoping to get some more information about her while we were here,"

Jasmine starts. "Is there anything you can tell us about the two of them?"

There is a pause. Runa places the photograph back onto the desk before answering. "The man in the photograph was one of the old caretakers of this lighthouse. And an inventor, too. His name was Desmond."

"Caretaker?" Jasmine asks.

"Yes, he took care of this lighthouse," Runa says.

"What's so important about this building?"

"Well, it was built long before the flooding happened. One of the last buildings still standing from before that time. We think it was part of an old communication network," Runa says.

"Is it functional?" I ask.

"Sadly, no. The tower hasn't been fully functional for centuries. Used to have electricity until a few months ago but even that's gone now. I know when Desmond lived here he was working on some big changes to it but none of the records have any mention of what he was actually working on," Runa says.

"What do you think it might have been?" Jasmine asks.

"The original documents for this place say it was supposed to be able to send signals all over the world. Some people speculated that it might even have been able to send signals further than that."

"Why would anyone need to send signals that far?" Jasmine asks.

"Who knows. And it's not like there are many people left to communicate with anymore," Runa says.

"That is unfortunate. We are searching for a power system, not a communication system," I say.

Jasmine picks up the photograph. "And who's the girl in the picture?"

"That was his daughter Olivia," Runa explains.

"What happened to them?"

"We don't really know. The records say that he abandoned the lighthouse and set up a new workshop north of June," Runa says. "When he left, he took most of his files with him. There's a pretty big gap in the history of the lighthouse from that time."

"Do you have the location of this new workshop?" I ask. Perhaps this workshop will contain relevant information regarding the power source he was constructing.

"Not exactly," Runa says.

"What do you mean?" Jasmine asks.

"The landscape north of here isn't easy to navigate. The only people that travel up that way are the nomads who live up past the ice fields."

"So how do we find the lab?" Jasmine asks.

"I wouldn't recommend it. There's a good chance you'll get lost out there without someone to guide you," Runa says.

"We must locate that lab," I say.

"Just be careful up there. It's really easy to get lost," Runa says. "And if the wind starts blowing there's nothing to stop it."

"We have to try either way," Jasmine says.

"I'm not gonna stop you. Just be careful going. Good luck to you both."

"Thanks for all your help," Jasmine says. I walk towards the door and leave the lighthouse. Jasmine follows closely behind me.

CHAPTER TEN

THE COTTAGE

The metal door of the lighthouse closes behind us and I walk along the stone path away from it.

"So where to next?" Jasmine asks.

"I am traveling north."

"Aren't you always?"

"I do not understand your question," I tell her.

"No, I just meant… It's a joke, Bit."

"I do not comprehend."

"Just that the whole time we've known each other you've been traveling north," she says.

"That is correct," I tell her.

"Never mind," she says, "I'm coming with you."

"I would not advise that course of action."

"Oh, and why not?"

"My body is capable of withstanding harsher conditions than yours. I also do not require food or water," I say.

"Counterpoint; so far since we've traveled together my body has held up just fine. In fact, I seem to remember carrying you a couple of miles."

"That is a fair analysis," I agree.

"You're not gonna stop me from coming."

"Then you can come," I tell her.

"Good, now let's go back to the inn and grab the rest of our supplies," Jasmine says. We walk back to the inn together and up to our room. Jasmine begins packing the supplies we had gathered and I check to make sure I have all of mine. I place the carved statue from Bruce back into my bag.

We leave the room, closing the door behind us, then walk down the wooden stairs and out of the inn. The woman from the front desk is still not around. We exit back onto the streets of June. The sun is now at its highest point in the sky and numerous people are out walking around the streets. Some have stopped to talk to each other, others walk quickly to their next destination.

Jasmine and I climb the stone steps up towards the top level of the town. The buildings in the upper levels are much smaller than the others in June. I stop at one of the streets.

"What's wrong?" Jasmine asks.

"I have seen this location before," I tell her.

"Where have you seen it?"

"It is in an early holo-recording."

"Wait, really?" Jasmine asks.

"Yes. Some features have changed, however the buildings are the same."

"So what was in that recording?"

"It was a documentation of the snow and a dinner with Ava and her family."

"Should we check it out?"

"There is no reason to."

"Why not?"

"The information contained in that holo-disc is not relevant to what we are attempting to discover."

"If you say so," she says as we continue up the steps. We reach the highest street level and Jasmine turns around to look out over the city. "It's really beautiful, don't you think?"

SUBROUTINE UPDATED – BEAUTY

"Yes, it does appear beautiful," I say.

Jasmine turns to face me. "So now you know what beauty is?" She laughs.

"I have been cataloging images as part of my beauty subroutine," I inform her.

"You know, Bit, you're pretty funny in your own way," Jasmine says.

"This has been told to me before." She smiles. We continue up the last set of stone steps. When we arrive at the top, there is a large carved wooden archway. There is also a strong breeze coming from the landscape in front of us. Next to the archway, there is a sign that reads, NOW LEAVING JUNE.

"Guess this is it, huh?" Jasmine says.

"What do you mean?" I ask.

"Beyond this is the ice fields. That's what Runa told us."

"We will discover what we are looking for," I tell her. We walk underneath the gate and onto the ice. I examine the landscape and there does not appear to be any landmarks or identifiable features of any kind. We walk forward and the ground crunches beneath my feet. The wind is blowing against us, slowing our speed by approximately twelve percent.

HARDWARE AT 84% INTEGRITY

After an hour of walking, I turn back around. I am still able to see the wooden archway in the distance. I turn forward again and continue. My internal temperature is falling in these conditions and Jasmine walks with her head down.

"Is your body at an adequate temperature?" I ask her.

"Yeah, let's just keep going," she says quickly. We continue and I keep my eyes on the horizon. If there are any variations, my eyes will be able to spot them long before Jasmine could. After another hour, I notice that while Jasmine has kept a consistent walking speed, my own has begun to decrease significantly.

"You doing ok there, Bit?" Jasmine asks from ahead of me.

SYSTEM DIAGNOSTIC STARTED

"I am still functioning," I tell her. "I have also begun a system diagnostic to determine why my walking speed has decreased."

"Well, let me know if you need to rest or something."

DIAGNOSTIC FINISHED – JOINT TEMPERATURE LOW

HARDWARE AT 83% INTEGRITY

Perhaps my system is not sufficiently optimized to maintain itself at such a low temperature. I will refrain from telling Jasmine until I run a second diagnostic later. The wind shifts direction and I see a spot of black on the horizon in front of us.

"That is the direction we must travel in." I point to the spot of black.

"How do you know?" Jasmine asks.

"There is an abnormality in the landscape. It is probable that there is an object of some kind in that location."

Jasmine looks to where I was pointing. "I don't see anything."

"My eyes have a higher range of vision."

"Ok, I trust you. Let's go." We alter our direction towards the new object on the horizon.

EYESIGHT FOCUSING

"The object appears to be a small building," I tell Jasmine.

"Wait, really? Do you think that could be what we're looking for?"

"I do not know."

"Well, if anything, it's a place to start, right?"

"That is correct," I tell her.

JOINT TEMPERATURE WARNING
HARDWARE AT 81% INTEGRITY

I continue walking anyway. I can feel my battery trying to reroute power to my joints to keep them heated. The electricity flowing through me begins to raise my body temperature. Jasmine looks over at me.

"Bit, there's steam rising off you!"

"My body is attempting to regulate the temperature in my joints." She puts down the bag of supplies and pulls out another shawl similar to the one she is wearing. She pulls the thick fabric around me.

"There, use this. Even you can freeze to death out here," she says.

"I am not capable of dying," I tell her.

"Yeah, sure. But you can stop working, right?"

"That is correct."

"Then it's kind of the same thing, right?"

"I do not believe so."

"Well, let's avoid it either way." After thirty-three more minutes, the object is within a clear visual range.

"Yeah you were right," Jasmine says. "It looks like some kind of small cottage."

We approach the cottage slowly. It appears to be constructed from dark wood and has a slanted roof. There is a large porch that wraps around the structure, also constructed from the same wood. There are spaces for windows, however they appear to have slabs of thick metal over them. There is a thick layer of ice covering most of the structure.

"Why would anyone build something this far out here?" Jasmine asks.

"I do not know." There does not seem to be any reason to construct a structure this far out of the way. We reach the cabin and I examine it more closely. The wood is not one I have ever seen before. I touch the wall, however my sensors do not appear to register it. Perhaps the cold is affecting them.

"Let's try to find the entrance," Jasmine says. We walk around the side of the building. The next side does not have any noticeable features apart from the porch. We continue to the far side of the cabin. On this side, there are steps up to a door with two large wooden columns on either side. I walk up to the door.

Upon inspection, it does not appear to have any mechanism to open it. Jasmine walks up and tries to push on the door. It does not move.

I examine the surroundings. Perhaps there is another mechanism to allow us entrance. Apart from the cabin, there does not appear to be any other structure around. I walk back to the door and place my hand on it. When I give the door a push, there is a whirring noise from inside the building.

"Something has been activated," I say. Jasmine steps back. There is a loud click and the door swings inwards. A light pours out.

"Should we go inside?" Jasmine asks.

"Yes," I say. We step into the cottage and the door swings closed behind us. The interior is decorated with brown wood paneling. There are a couple of small bookshelves on the walls, and sofas surrounding a glass table.

"It's not really what I was expecting," Jasmine says. She walks over to an old clock on the wall. It appears to be functioning.

"Let us look around," I say. I browse through the books on the bookshelf. *Brick Oven Pizza. Practical Guide to Ice Fishing. 22nd Century Art History Retrospective.* None of the titles here relate remotely to what we are looking for. Nothing about the grid or electrical systems. No information about what Desmond had been working on.

"Hey, Bit!" I hear Jasmine call from the other room. I put down a book and join her. She points to a portrait on the wall. "It's her again, isn't it?" I examine the portrait. The person appears to be me.

"That is Olivia," I say.

"Yeah I know, I just can't get over why she looks like you."

"That is not relevant to our search."

Jasmine shakes her head. "I'm not entirely sure that that's true, though."

"I do not understand."

"Well, you just happened to have these holo-recordings handed down to you by someone. And then you try to track down the father of this girl in the recordings to find some power source to fix the grid system," she says.

"I do not—"

"And then you find out that his daughter and you have the exact same face? I'm sorry but it's just too big of a coincidence. Something is happening here. How else do you explain it?" Jasmine asks.

"I do not know."

"Like, what are even the chances that those holo-recordings would have found you?"

RUNNING PROBABILITY

"It is highly improbable," I say.

"That's exactly what I'm talking about," Jasmine says. "And now there's another portrait of you, or her, here! Like, it doesn't make any sense to me. And I won't leave until I know what's going on."

"That is acceptable."

Jasmine sighs and continues to walk around the house. I follow alongside her. We walk into a small kitchen area with cabinets along the walls and I open one of them. Inside is a shelf of preserved foods. Jasmine opens another to find the same thing.

"Well, remind me to stock up before we leave," says Jasmine.

REMINDER SET – STOCK UP

"I have set a reminder to remind you to stock up before we leave." She laughs and walks out of the kitchen into another room. The walls of the next room are lined with more books.

"You know, I was just thinking about what you said back in the tavern," she says.

"To what are you referring?"

"About coming with you to stay in Valentine. After we find the power source, I think I'm gonna do that." She walks over to a door on the other side of the room and opens it up. Inside is a staircase leading down. "Let's see what's down here," she says.

She walks down the staircase and I follow. At the bottom is a small landing with another door. Similar to the metal door out-side, this one does not have any mechanisms attached to it. There is a small panel to the side of the doorway with a handprint on it. Jasmine places her hand onto the panel. There is a soft buzzing noise and the panel turns red.

"Well that didn't seem to work." She pauses. "I have an idea, you give it a try." I walk over and place my hand onto the panel. There is a ding as it lights up green. The door swings inwards.

"The door is open," I say.

"Yeah, and that's too much of a coinci-dence if you ask me. There's absolutely something going on here." She quickly walks through the door into the room beyond. I step through behind her.

The room is a mess. There are papers stacked throughout on large wooden desks. The walls are likewise covered with papers and drawings. Old blackboards lean up against the walls. The room is large and seems to stretch on for a much longer dis-tance than the house above it does.

"Now this is a little more of what I was expecting," Jasmine says as she walks further into the room.

"There is a lot of information to process here." I begin to scan the drawings and texts pinned along the walls. My eyes stop when they reach a spot on the floor. I recognize it instantly as the door that Ava and Olivia had climbed through in the holo-recording. Jasmine catches me staring at it and walks over.

"That's the same hatch, isn't it?" she asks.

"That is correct," I tell her. I bend down to examine the door. The metal has been fused together around the opening.

"Doesn't look like we can open that," Jasmine says.

"The entrance has been sealed."

"I'm going to say it again, there's no way this is all a coincidence. Like, even the fact that this cottage exists here can't be a coincidence."

"The most logical explanation is that the cabin was constructed here after the discovery of this hatch."

"Wait, really?"

"Yes. In the recording there was no evidence of this structure," I explain.

"Oh yeah, I guess that makes sense."

"Olivia says in the recording that she told her father about this location as well," I say, "and based on the information we received at the lighthouse, that must be when Desmond left and moved to this location."

"But I still have so many questions."

"I do too," I tell her. I stand up from the hatch in the floor and continue to search the room. I open a cupboard and find the head of another android that looks identical to mine.

"What the hell is that?" Jasmine says when she sees it.

"It would appear to be my face." I examine the head. Cables and wires are coming out from the bottom of the neck. There is also a panel open at the side of the head. In the rest of the cabinet are various other parts I recognize from my own internal mechanisms.

"What is all this?"

"This is an android," I tell her.

"I don't understand."

I notice a small box inside the cabinet, which I open. Inside are three holo-discs.

"There are holo-recorder discs." I pull the holo-recorder out of my bag and open the top. I place the first disc into the recorder and turn the device on. An image appears in front of me. It is the face of Olivia's father, Desmond. He is standing in the same room Jasmine and I currently stand in.

"Journal Entry 33892-PD. The construction around here has just finished. We built this lab from the same material as the ship. It should be able to hold up against anything that may happen," Desmond says. *"I also built us a little cabin above the lab to stay in. Much roomier than that lighthouse."*

"He sounds excited," Jasmine says.

"My daughter Olivia found this place while she was exploring with that girlfriend of hers. I don't think she has any idea just what she stumbled on here." Desmond pauses. *"I barely understand what we have here. But one thing I do know is that whatever was happening here was far beyond any technology that I have seen before. And I may have finally found an answer to the problem I've been having with Wardenclyffe."* He steps aside and shows a drawing of the lighthouse.

"When we learned that the grid was going to fail, we tried everything we could think of. But the answer was unfortunately clear; the grid isn't going to last. We still don't know when or what exactly will cause it. But I needed to find some solution for it." Desmond looks at the drawing of Wardenclyffe again. *"Then I had the idea; what if we could use the same technology Wardenclyffe uses to broadcast signals around the world to broadcast electricity instead?"*

"Wait, is that even possible?" Jasmine asks.

"I do not know," I say. This technology is unlike any I have heard of before.

"I spent years renovating the lighthouse, getting it ready. But the one fatal flaw to this problem was that I did not have any power source for my invention. All my prototypes just weren't powerful enough... until now."

He moves the camera to the left, revealing the hatch in the ground fully open. *"Deep down there, we found the power source we've been looking for. We just have to find a way to get it out and install it into the lighthouse. With that, we should be able to bring the power back online everywhere,"* he explains. The recording ends.

"That is the solution," I say. "We simply require that power source."

"But where is it?" Jasmine asks. "Do you think it's still down there?" She points to the door in the ground.

"There is a probability of that," I tell her.

"Let's watch the next recording, then. Maybe one of these has the answer," Jasmine says. I open the holo-recorder and switch to the next recording. Desmond appears in the air, this time he appears very different. His beard is no longer trimmed, his hair is long and unkempt. He is in the same location, however it looks much less organized.

"He looks horrible," Jasmine says.

"Journal Entry 33893-whatever. So, Olivia's dead," Desmond says. There are tears in his eyes. *"I haven't been able to bring myself to work on the Wardenclyffe project anymore. Probably wouldn't have worked anyway. I've decided to try a new project for a bit."* He reaches out and turns the camera around. I see myself lying on the table. *"I*

may not be able to bring her back, but I can do the next best thing."

"Wait, is that you?" Jasmine asks.

"I do not know," I tell her. My brain is attempting to connect the information that I already know with these new pieces.

"I took one of those old androids and gave it a couple of upgrades. It may not be Olivia, but I'm hoping it will keep her memory alive… at least a bit," Desmond says. *"I tried to write a program to give it personality, make it as human as possible. And I think I found a solution to the power issues I was having with the prototypes."* He holds up a glowing red object.

"That is my internal battery." I recognize the part instantly.

"Wait, what?" Jasmine asks. Desmond cuts her off before she can talk more.

"We finally got that damn power source out from down there. It had grown almost completely into the structure," Desmond says, pointing to the hatch again. *"And I figure why waste it on Wardenclyffe? Why not put it to much better use?"* He walks over to me on the table and opens the panel on my chest. I watch as he attaches the battery into my chest cavity. There is a whirring noise from the recording. *"There we go. And just like that, she should never run out of power. Hell, she'll probably be the last functioning*

thing on this planet long after we're gone. I just wanted to keep a bit of her alive." He begins to cry. *"Olivia..."* The recording cuts off.

"So does that mean what I think it does?" Jasmine asks.

My system finally connects the information and finishes processing. "The power source that we have been looking for is my internal battery," I say.

"I don't understand how that's possible."

"That explains why I am the last currently operating android. My design has an optimized power source that the other androids did not."

"And why you look like Olivia?"

"I was constructed in her image by Desmond after Olivia passed away," I say. There is a comfort to having all the information processed in my mind.

"But what about how you ended up in Valentine?" Jasmine asks.

"I do not have the answer to that query."

Jasmine pulls the last holo-disc from the box. "Let's see if we can get one last answer," she says as she presses play on the holo-recorder. Desmond's image appears again. He is older than the previous recording. The background is from the room upstairs.

"I don't know who's ever going to watch this recording. I just sent Bit away from here.

That's what I ended up calling the android," Desmond says. *"I thought it would be a comfort having someone like my daughter here again. But the only thing it did was remind me that she was gone. I couldn't even bring myself to call her Olivia. I didn't have the heart to deactivate her, but I also couldn't bear to keep her around."* He stops and puts his head into his hands. *"I reset her memory, everything about June, Wardenclyffe, Olivia, all of it. I sent her away to Ava. I didn't know where else to send her. I don't even know if she'd want Bit, but I just had to do something."* He looks up into the camera. There are tears in his eyes again. *"And if somehow you ever see this, Bit, I just want you to know how sorry I am."* He stops. *"If you're the last one out there, I hope you can manage to keep the memory of us humans alive. I know we weren't perfect, but there were some truly beautiful moments."*

SUBROUTINE UPDATED – BEAUTY

He stops speaking and then the recording stops. I place the holo-recorder down on the table.

"So now what do we do?" asks Jasmine.

"I do not know," I answer.

WARDENCLYFFE

Jasmine and I walk up the stairs back into the main level of the cottage. Neither of us speaks. Jasmine walks towards the kitchen and grabs food from the cabinets. I walk into the living room and sit down on the couch. After a few minutes, Jasmine finds me and sits down. She has a large plate of food in her hand.

"I realized I hadn't eaten in a couple of hours." She quietly eats the rest of her meal. When she puts the plate on the glass table in front of us it clinks loudly. "You know, I was so preoccupied I didn't even really think about it, but how does this place have electricity?"

"I do not know." I pause. "I also do not know what the best course of action is."

Jasmine laughs. "Well I'm glad you don't either. That was a lot of information to take in."

"Even for me, the information was a large amount to process," I assure her.

"Does it feel better to know?" she asks.

"Yes."

"Really?"

"Yes, my operating system runs more efficiently when I do not have to run background processes. These questions have been occupying my mind for a considerable time," I say.

"That must feel nice." We sit in silence for another minute before she speaks again. "So have you given any more thought to what you're gonna do?"

"I have not yet determined that."

"Are we going back to June?"

SYSTEM ANALYZING

"Yes, there is no further purpose in staying here," I tell her.

"Well, let me get all my stuff together then we can go."

REMINDER ACTIVATED – STOCK UP

"I would also like to remind you to remember to 'stock up' before we leave."

She laughs. "Good memory, Bit!" Jasmine goes into the kitchen and I hear her opening cabinets in there. I walk around the room and examine the objects, cataloging them before leaving. I place my bag onto my shoulder as Jasmine finishes in the kitchen and comes back out with the bag much fuller than before we had arrived.

"Shall we go?" she asks.

"Yes." I open the front door and step out of the cabin. The landscape is still flat and empty, however now the wind has subsided.

"Do you know which direction it is?" Jasmine asks.

"Yes. My internal compass is perfectly accurate," I tell her. Another memory clicks in my mind. "The typical android does not possess directional systems," I tell Jasmine.

"Oh really?"

"This must be an additional feature that was given to me by Desmond."

Jasmine and I step off the porch back onto the snow. We begin to walk south, back towards June. Without the wind hindering our movement, we are able to complete the journey in approximately one hour and nineteen minutes less than our previous trip north. I see the gate to June in the distance.

SYSTEM ERROR

HARDWARE AT 75% INTEGRITY

"The gate to June is ahead," I say to Jasmine. She looks up.

"Oh yeah, I see it,"

SYSTEM OVERCLOCKED

HARDWARE AT 70% INTEGRITY

I stop walking. The error is becoming more persistent.

"Why did you stop?" Jasmine asks.

"My system is running over its capacity."

"What does that mean?"

"If my analysis is correct, there is a high probability that my system was not designed to operate outside of such regular parameters."

"I don't understand."

"The power source appears to be unstable," I say.

"How long has this been happening?" Jasmine asks.

"Since my system was overloaded with the lightning strike," I say.

"But that was back when I first found you! Why didn't you say anything?"

"I was attempting to run a diagnostic test. However, with this new information, this may no longer be sufficient."

"So how much longer do you have?"

"Unknown," I tell her.

SYSTEM RESTORED

I begin walking towards June again.

"So what are you going to do?" she asks running after me.

"I will run probabilities for multiple scenarios to determine the best outcome," I tell her. We arrive back at the gate to June. The city appears unchanged.

"So where should we go first now that we're back?"

"We should travel to the Wardenclyffe Lighthouse." We walk down the steps into the city and continue downwards. We arrive at the level that the lighthouse is on and turn onto the stone street. As we approach, I look up at the dome on top of it.

MEMORY RETRIEVED

I recall the blueprints from the wall of Desmond's workshop of the Wardenclyffe tower. He has wired everything through the top floor of the building.

We arrive at the door and step inside. Runa is waiting and rushes over to greet us.

"Did you two actually go onto the ice shelf up there?" she asks.

"That is correct," I tell her.

"Wow, you two are gutsy, I'll give you that. Glad you made it back in one piece," she says.

"Do you mind if we sit for a bit?" Jasmine asks.

"Oh no, not at all! Where are my manners? Let me grab you poor things some chairs." She walks over to the other side of the room and comes back with two large chairs, placing them in front of the hearth. Jasmine and I walk over and sit down.

"Thank you," Jasmine says.

"So you two wanna tell me what you found out there?" Runa asks.

"We discovered the location of the professor's workshop," I tell her.

"Really? Well I'll be."

"That is correct," I say.

"We also figured out what he was doing to Wardenclyffe Lighthouse," Jasmine says.

"And what was that?"

"It was a new power system. Designed to replace the grid."

"How would that even be possible?"

"The system was designed to wirelessly transmit energy across the planet," I tell her.

"What happened to it?" Runa asks. Jasmine yawns. "Oh wow. You two are probably exhausted and here I am drilling you with all these questions. Let me get out of your hair. You are welcome to stay here as long as you like, ok? And if you need me, I'll be right upstairs," Runa says as she climbs up the spiral staircase.

Shortly after Runa goes upstairs, Jasmine is asleep in the chair. I stand up and walk around the room. The walls are all coated in a series of wires. I walk up to one and examine them. The cables come out of the floor and go directly up the wall through the ceiling. I place my hand on the cables. There is no electricity running through any of them. I have not observed electricity anywhere in June.

I pick up the photograph of Desmond and Olivia again. I examine her face. As much as she shares my appearance, I cannot connect with her. Perhaps that stems from my lack of emotions or the fact that she and I are separate entities. She is smiling wide in the photo. I stretch my face to match hers yet it does not provoke any response in my coding.

"You know, I don't think I've ever seen you smile before." I turn around and see Jasmine awake again.

"You are not asleep." I place the photograph back onto the table.

"Yeah, couldn't stay asleep."

"You require rest." I sit down in the chair next to her.

"Tell me more about what it's like back in Valentine," she says, before yawning.

"Is there specific information you would like to hear about?"

"Not particularly, just tell me about it."

"Valentine has two-hundred-and-eighty-two residents and is approximately thirty square kilometers," I say.

"You really paint quite a picture."

QUERY – PAINT A PICTURE

"In what way am I painting a picture?" I ask.

"No, I was just joking. I'm too tired to explain it right now." She closes her eyes. "When I wake up you can tell me all about it. Or on our trip back." She falls asleep again. I look around the room at all the books and papers stacked along the bookshelves and desks.

I get up from the chair again and pull out papers from one desk. *June census year 2572.* The paper contains a list of names and addresses. I place it back onto the desk and pull out a book from the shelf. *The grid: a modern-day power system.* The book is old and worn out. The pages are faded significantly. I close the book and place it back onto the shelf, before turning toward the fireplace. Jasmine is still asleep in the chair and I sit down opposite her.

After many hours, the sun begins to come through the windows of the lighthouse. It shines on Jasmine's face and she stirs awake.

"How long was I asleep?" she asks.

"You were asleep for approximately eight hours and thirty-one minutes," I tell her.

"Oh wow, so a while this time?"

"That is correct."

Runa walks down the staircase and greets us. "Good morning, you two! How did you both sleep?"

"I do not require sleep," I inform her.

"I, on the other hand, slept incredibly well, thank you," Jasmine says.

"Oh I'm so happy to hear it."

"Runa," I say.

"Yes?"

"Will you show me to the top level of the lighthouse, please?"

She looks surprised. "Of course, but why would you want to go up there?"

"I memorized the blueprints of this place when I was in Desmond's lab. I believe there is something I can do to activate this tower."

"Wait, really?" Jasmine asks.

"That is correct."

"Well let's get you up there, then!" Runa says. She waves her hand at Jasmine and I as she leads us to the spiral staircase. We climb up and emerge on the next level of the lighthouse. This level appears very similar to the one below it. The walls are coated in wires and there are a number of organized bookshelves and desks with neatly stacked papers. We climb to the next level, which appears to be a living space.

"Do you live here?" Jasmine asks.

"Of course I do! All the lighthouse caretakers live here. Even Desmond lived in here for a time," Runa says.

"It's a cute place," Jasmine says. "Reminds me of my place back home."

"Well you're welcome to stay here as long as you want to," Runa says.

"I might take you up on that before we head out." We pass quickly through the level. The next two have a similar appearance to Desmond's lab.

"Were these levels designed by Desmond?" I ask.

Runa nods. "I'm afraid so, they don't get too much use these days, though."

We arrive at the second-to-last level and the spiral staircase ends. The cables from around the walls all converge in the center of this room. Along the walls are two large staircases.

"What're all the wires here for?" Jasmine asks.

"It's hard to tell anymore. I think some have been here since the beginning," Runa says as she steps over a bundle of cables and walks towards one of the staircases. "I think some of the others were added by Desmond."

We walk up the staircase and arrive at the top level of the lighthouse. It is a large spherical glass room. The walls seem to be constructed from large beams of metal with thick glass triangles between them. Around the entire room are massive white statues. They appear to be made from the same white stone as the lighthouse itself. On the base of each statue is a metal plaque. I read the names; Jupiter, Juno, Vesta.

I stop in front of the plaque that reads Mercury and examine the statue. I reach into my bag and remove the carved figure given to me by Bruce. The two figures are identical. Jasmine walks up to me.

"Wait, are those the same figure?"

"That is correct," I tell her.

"You know, I feel like every time we get an answer to something, it just gives us ten more questions," she says. I keep the figure in my hand as I turn around. In the center of the room, across from the statue, is a large door that is sitting open. Inside the door is a seat with cables connected to it.

"So what exactly are we doing up here, Bit?" Jasmine asks.

"I spent the night running probabilities to determine a solution for the power system," I say.

"Did you find anything?"

"Yes."

"Wait, really? That's great!"

"I have reached a decision about how to fix the power," I tell her.

"So what is it?"

"I am the solution," I say. She does not respond. "And this tower," I continue.

"I don't understand."

"The only way to activate this tower is by using my power source," I tell her. Jasmine is silent for a couple of seconds.

HARDWARE AT 68% INTEGRITY

"Wait, no! There must be another way!" Jasmine grabs onto my arm. "I'm not gonna let you do that!"

"I have run every possible outcome to this scenario. The new power system is fully integrated into Wardenclyffe according to Desmond's blueprints." I remove her arm from around mine.

"I won't accept that!" Jasmine says. "You've come all this way! There has to be another way to fix it, right? What about looking for a new power source?"

"There is no record of another power source," I say.

"Can't they get by without power? Other places are doing it!"

"I have given my word that I would locate a power source for them."

"What's that matter? This is your life that we're talking about!"

"I am not alive," I remind her.

"Oh, come on, you're more human than most people I know!" she yells.

"My hardware is also failing," I tell her.

"Why didn't you say anything? We could've tried to fix you!"

"The damage has progressed past the point of repair."

HARDWARE AT 60% INTEGRITY

"What about carrying on the memory of the human race? What about outlasting everything on this planet?" she asks.

"My system is not designed to operate at this capacity. If I do nothing I will not continue to function," I explain.

"I don't want to lose you!"

"I am afraid that there is no scenario where I shall continue to function for more than another month."

"But what about me? You're just gonna leave me alone?" Jasmine asks. "I thought we were going to go on adventures together."

"I am afraid this is where my adventure will cease," I tell her.

There are tears in her eyes. Runa puts her arm around Jasmine. "There, there, dear."

"Runa, may I ask you one favor?"

"Of course, what do you need?"

"Do not let her stop me." I step through the door into the room beyond and it closes behind me. Jasmine breaks away from Runa and rushes to the glass window of the door. She bangs her hands against it.

"Don't you dare do this, Bit!" she yells through the glass. I take a seat on the chair inside the room and open the panel on my chest. The red glow from my power unit fills the room. I grab the cable from one side of the chair in one hand.

"What about going back to Valentine together?" she yells.

I grab the opposite cable in the other hand and slowly raise them up to either side of the power unit in my chest.

"Where am I supposed to go next?"

I touch the cables to my power unit and instantly feel a spark as the heat of the electricity flowing through the wires melts the cables into my chest.

SYSTEM ERROR

I feel my power begin to drain from all essential systems.

FATAL ERROR. HARDWARE AT 50% INTEGRITY

My arms drop to my side.

MEMORY COMPROMISED

I can no longer recall all of my memories. I can feel the lighthouse systems booting up around me as my power drains. I hear a voice in my head.

WARDENCLYFFE LIGHTHOUSE SYSTEMS ACTIVE

SIGNAL ONLINE

My systems continue to shut down one by one.

SYSTEMS OFFLINE

BEAUTY SUBROUTINE ACTIVATED

My subroutine activates itself as the rest of my systems shut down.

MEMORIES RETRIEVED

"Come back soon, ok?" I see Neil's face in my memory.

"And don't you wait too long before visiting me again," Mary's voice says.

"Thank you so much for this, Bit." Edna's face flashes into my memory next.

"It's a good thing, Bit! It's all a good change," Bruce's voice says.

"And don't worry, we'll keep things just the same here for you," Kit says from the gates of Paradise with Roger.

"Goodbye, Bit. With any luck, we'll meet again someday," I hear Rupert's voice as he steps onto the *Elizabeth.*

"Sometimes it's about memories. Like something is beautiful because it reminds us of a happy memory," Jasmine's voice says last. My mind continues to replay my memories as it shuts down.

DATABASE UPDATED – BEAUTY

BEAUTY SUBROUTINE ANALYSIS COMPLETED

I look through the window of the room. I see Jasmine's face looking in at me. I remember the times that we spent traveling together. As I see the statue through the window in front of me, my memories of the fountain in Valentine surface. I recall the times spent there with all the residents. I look down at the carved statue in my hand.

"It's beautiful," I say as my last systems continue to shut down.

PHYSICAL SYSTEMS TERMINATED

My hands go limp as my hardware shuts down. The figure falls out of my hand.
HARDWARE AT 21% INTEGRITY
END PROCESS
SYSTEM FATAL ERROR
SYSTEM OSOLIVE2410 ARCHIVED
END PROGRAM

Acknowledgements

It's been said many times that no one accomplishes anything alone, and this novel is a testament to that. So many people helped this book get to where it is today and for that I am eternally grateful.

Beginning with my mother, who raised me on the most incredible stories and instilled in me a love of storytelling. I would not be where I am in life without your guidance and love.

I have to thank my teachers who helped teach me how to write and find my own voice as an author. Whether that was stories about pumpkins from when I was in kindergarten or short stories in high school that were entirely unrelated to the class assignments. I'd like to thank my fifth grade teacher Mr. Solomon who brought books to life by reading them to our class and taught me how a good story can stick with you for your entire life.

I'd also like to thank my writing group, The Splotches, for helping to turn this story from an inkling of an idea into something more complete. The feedback each of you provided made this story what it is today and I miss you all so much.

This novella would not be what it is without the help of my editor, Jess Lawrence who helped me polish up the story and get it ready for the rest of the world to see.

Thank you to Minna Ollikainen for your incredible interior illustrations and to Abigail Spence for the beautiful cover art. Both of you helped capture the feeling of the story perfectly through your art.

Lastly I would like to thank you, the person reading this. As a self published author, it means so much to have someone read my story. I truly hope, from the bottom of my heart, that you enjoy reading it as much as I enjoyed writing it.

ABOUT THE AUTHOR

Lloyd Hall is a writer from Branford, CT. In addition to writing, he has a background as a Fashion Designer and Costumer. He has a strong love of hats and puns. Wardenclyffe is his first published novel.

www.lloyd-parker-hall.com